"You're too inexperienced."

Whitney snorted her skepticism. "At the picnic, you were full of talk about sizzle and volcanoes. Now suddenly I'm too inexperienced?"

"Sizzle is a quality," Dean said tightly. "It isn't practical experience."

She threw up her hands in exasperation. "You beat everything! How am I supposed to get experience if you keep bird-dogging me? This isn't exactly a spectator sport we're talking about here."

He was staring at the ceiling again, his expression closed. "Who taught you how to play baseball?" he asked, his voice abrupt.

"You did."

"Who taught you how to ride a bicycle? To drive a car? To throw a dirty punch in a fight?"

"We both know you taught me all those things. So what's your point?" she asked in frustration.

Dean turned his head slowly to meet her eyes. She stared at him in irritated confusion until, suddenly, the truth broke through....

Dear Reader,

Welcome to Silhouette **Special Edition** . . . welcome to romance. Each month, Silhouette **Special Edition** publishes six novels with you in mind—stories of love and life, tales that you can identify with—romance with that little "something special" added in.

We've got a celebration going here this month! We're introducing a brand-new cover design for Silhouette **Special Edition.** We hope you like our new look, as well as our six wonderful books this month. We're pleased to present you with Nora Roberts's exciting new series— THE DONOVAN LEGACY. *Captivated* is the first tale, and it's full of magical love galore! The next books, *Entranced* and *Charmed,* will be heading your way in October and November. Don't miss these enchanting tales!

And rounding out this month are books from other exciting authors: Judi Edwards, Marie Ferrarella, Billie Green, Phyllis Halldorson and Betsy Johnson.

In each Silhouette **Special Edition** novel, we're dedicated to bringing you the romances that you dream about— stories that will delight as well as bring a tear to the eye. And that's what Silhouette **Special Edition** is all about— special books by special authors for special readers!

I hope you enjoy this book and all of the stories to come.

Sincerely,

Tara Gavin
Senior Editor
Silhouette Books

BILLIE GREEN

THAT BOY FROM TRASH TOWN

SPECIAL EDITION

Published by Silhouette Books New York

America's Publisher of Contemporary Romance

SILHOUETTE BOOKS
300 East 42nd St., New York, N.Y. 10017

THAT BOY FROM TRASH TOWN

Copyright © 1992 by Billie Green

All rights reserved. Except for use in any review, the reproduction or utilization of this work in whole or in part in any form by any electronic, mechanical or other means, now known or hereafter invented, including xerography, photocopying and recording, or in any information storage or retrieval system, is forbidden without the permission of the publisher, Silhouette Books, 300 E. 42nd St., New York, N.Y. 10017

ISBN: 0-373-09763-8

First Silhouette Books printing September 1992

Books by Billie Green

Silhouette Special Edition

Jesse's Girl #297
A Special Man #346
Voyage of the Nightingale #379
Time After Time #415
That Boy From Trash Town #763

Silhouette Books

Silhouette Summer Sizzlers 1988
"The Image of a Girl"

BILLIE GREEN's

college professor once told her that she was a *natural* writer. But her readers and editors find it hard to believe that she writes one good story after another only because she comes by them naturally. Maybe someday this devoted wife, mother of three and romance writer *extraordinaire* will create a heroine who is a writer. Then, possibly, we will get a hint of her trials and tribulations.

Chapter One

"Alvo...Alvo, listen— Damn it, kid, would you shut up and listen for a minute!"

Assured that he had finally gained the fifteen-year-old's attention, Dean leaned back in his chair and let his shoulders relax a little. "I'm your lawyer," he said slowly, calmly. "And what's more important, I outweigh you by at least fifty pounds. Be smart for once in your life and listen to me. I don't care if the guards are a bunch of retarded sleazes like you say. They're in control, Alvo. They have the power. Fight them and you'll only hurt yourself. Word is, they're ready to start pumping you full of Ritalin. So unless you can fake them into believing you're a civilized member of— What? What did you say?"

When Alvo repeated his opinion of civilization, Dean laughed. "You have a warped sense of humor, kid. I like that. But I'm afraid my opinion isn't shared by the guardians of the law who have to put up with you on a daily basis. Come on now, you've got a brain. Use it. Let me do my job without worrying about whether or not you're terrorizing your fellow inmates."

But Alvo wasn't ready to give up yet. It took Dean another thirty minutes to get a grudging promise of good behavior from the boy. It would do for now, he told himself as he hung up the phone, even though he was pretty sure his idea of good behavior was nowhere near his young client's.

Alvo Gutierrez was accused of brutally assaulting his stepfather, Harland Jackson. On the surface the whole thing looked cut-and-dried—everyone who knew the boy said Alvo had a violent temper. From his hospital bed, Jackson swore that his stepson had attacked him, beating him senseless because he refused to give Alvo money for drugs.

The boy's story was tragic, but unfortunately not unusual. Dean had handled plenty of similar cases—men, women and children who turned against their own families in an explosive act of violence.

To make things worse, Alvo wasn't exactly a physically attractive specimen. His thin face was pitted with acne scars, his hair habitually dirty. And his personality was even worse. With his foul mouth and bad temper, Alvo offended anyone who came in contact with him.

Only twice in the two weeks that he had worked with him had Dean caught a glimpse of the real Alvo Gutierrez. There was something in his eyes, something scared and lonely. It was that boy who Dean was busting his butt to help. It was the scared, lonely boy behind the belligerent act who Dean refused to give up on. He would have done his best on the case no matter what the circumstances, but that rare glimpse of the real Alvo was pushing him to go the extra mile. There was also the fact that, although there was no physical resemblance, Alvo reminded Dean of himself at that age. And Dean, of all people, knew what it felt like to be scared and lonely.

Pushing away from his desk, he stood up and moved to pull a heavy law book from the bookshelves lining one wall of his home office. Thumbing through it, he looked for a case he vaguely remembered from law school.

When he eventually found it, Dean read through it slowly, even though he was pretty sure it was a waste of time and wouldn't be relevant to the case at hand. He was deeply into judicial doublespeak when a slight noise pulled his attention away from his work.

Looking up, Dean saw the head and right half of a young woman more or less hanging around the doorjamb. She wore a faded green T-shirt and ragged cutoff jeans. Her black, shoulder-length hair was pulling loose from a careless ponytail, and her blue eyes sparkled with some irresistibly exuberant emotion—amusement, perhaps, or excitement—that added to the look of beautiful vagabond.

A stranger observing them would probably have thought that Dean, the respectable, affluent lawyer, had befriended a young woman from the wrong side of the tracks.

The idea almost made Dean laugh. Whitney Grant was twenty-four and had just received a graduate degree in Art History. Her mother, Anne Harcourt Grant, was one of *the* San Antonio Harcourts, very important people in this neck of the woods.

Although most of her revered relatives were all flash and no substance, Whitney was a different breed of Harcourt. When the occasion called for it, she had enough flash to dazzle a blind man, but on the inside, where it counted, Whitney was true-blue.

"Dean, my Dean," she said earnestly, her generous lips curving in an outrageous grin. "Did I ever tell you you're my one and only true friend?"

He closed the law book and studied her grin with suspicious eyes. "You're making me nervous, Whitney," he said finally. "Come on, get it over with. Have you murdered one of your cousins? All of them? Did you incite the Harcourt servants to riot? What?"

Her eyes widened in what he knew from experience was plainly false indignation. "You wound me. I don't know what you're talking about."

"I'm talking about whatever it is you're hiding on the other side of that door."

"Oh, *this*."

Turning, she began to back into the room, exposing the end of a rope that was clutched between both her hands. Whatever was attached to the other end obviously didn't want to come in, but that didn't stop Whitney. She struggled and pulled, slipped and slid, then turned around with the rope over her shoulder and leaned forward. Finally an enormous dog—at least Dean thought it was a dog—skidded on its rump across the polished wood floor.

"Happy birthday, Dean," Whitney said, trying to catch her breath. "Isn't he wonderful? The perfect gift. Are you surprised? I wanted to—"

"My birthday's in November," he said, staring with morbid fascination at the animal who was now in the process of off-loading fleas.

Whitney shot a glance at Dean. "Oh, well, I knew that of course, but I was hoping you wouldn't remember. How would you feel about an early Bastille Day gift? Please, Dean. Forget how he looks and try to see the inner dog. He's loaded with personality. I call him Oscar because he has kind of a wild look, and I thought something literary would give him a little dignity. Oscar Wilde... get it? I found him just wandering around by the stables. Uncle Ames would have told somebody to shoot him, and Mother would have had nineteen different kinds of fits if I had tried to keep him. So what do you think?" she said, ending on a hopeful note.

This wasn't the first stray Whitney had brought to Dean, and knowing her, it probably wouldn't be the last. He ran his gaze over her beautiful face, intending to tell her to remove the offensive animal from the premises. But as usual he found himself caught, trapped by the charm that surrounded her like a bright haze.

"Pete Watkins down the street has been talking about getting his boy a dog," he said slowly. "I'm pretty sure Pete had a spaniel or collie in mind—something recognizably canine—but I'll show them this...this *thing*. There's not a boy alive who could resist a dog that ugly." Dean frowned and sniffed the air. "Have you been feeding him pepperoni?"

With a tiny squeal of pleasure, she threw her arms around Dean's neck. "I knew you'd help me. You can tell he hasn't had a home for a while, poor thing."

Dean untangled himself from her arms. "He doesn't deserve a home. He doesn't deserve a life. And if he lifts his leg by my desk, he won't have one. Now get out and take that thing with you. I have work to do."

Dean watched her leave, pulling the obstinate animal behind her, then he turned back to his work. But concentrating on his work wasn't that easy. His mind kept wandering. Whitney always had this effect on him, damn her.

In Dean's backyard, Whitney tied Oscar to a tree, and filled a plastic bucket with water, placing it close enough for the dog to reach it when he was thirsty. Then she sneaked back into the kitchen and began looking through the contents of Dean's pantry. After a moment she pulled out a large can of beef stew and opened it, using a manual can opener instead of the electric one so Dean wouldn't hear.

She had written an IOU on the pad by the telephone and was tiptoeing out the back door, when she heard, "You better not be feeding my T-bone to that mutt!"

Laughing, she closed the door behind her.

As Oscar ate, Whitney looked around Dean's backyard. It was a small yard, and Dean made sure it was kept neat and clean, like his house. But like his house, it was just a bit utilitarian: precisely trimmed grass, symmetrically clipped hedge. There was nothing in the yard that was just for the sake of aesthetics.

The dog was lapping up the last bit of gravy when Dean walked out the back door and sat down on the stoop. His dark brown hair was slightly tousled, as though he had been running his fingers through it, and his brown eyes looked tired.

There was a French grandfather somewhere in Dean's family tree, and he had inherited the dark complexion, the compelling features. Although it was only April, he was already tanned, but Dean always tanned early. It was as though any available sunlight waited for this particular body to land on, which was perfectly understandable to Whitney. If a sunbeam had any discrimination at all it would want to touch Dean.

He wasn't the most handsome man Whitney had ever met. At least, he wasn't pretty in the way most of the men she knew tried to be. But he was far and away the most attractive. There was something about his strong features, something about his dark Gallic eyes, that made a woman profoundly aware that she was a woman.

After disposing of the empty stew can, she joined the object of her thoughts on the stoop and tilted her head to examine his features. There was something in his expression—worry or disillusionment—that made her want to put her arms around him and comfort him. But she knew she wouldn't. It wasn't allowed. Dean had some kind of industrial-strength masculine gene that kept him from admitting to any kind of weakness. Even the need for human companionship.

After a while he turned and met her eyes. "Why are you so quiet?" he asked suspiciously.

She laughed. "You looked like you were doing some heavy-duty thinking. I didn't want to interrupt the genius at work." She paused. "The Gutierrez case not going well?"

"Not going, period. The boy won't talk. He admits he attacked his stepfather and that he knew what he was doing at the time." He shook his head. "But something's wrong with the whole setup. I can feel it. There was no trace of drugs in his system. No indication at all that he's the heavy user Jackson—that's his stepfather—says he is. If Alvo were desperate for a fix, so desperate that he'd beat a man's brains out to get them, there would be signs, Whitney. Withdrawal isn't something you can hide that easily."

"So the stepfather's lying," she said. "And if he lied about that, he could have lied about other things, as well. What does the mother say?"

"Nothing that helps. She says she was at the supermarket when Alvo attacked her husband, but the woman is barely functional. She's scared, or in shock, or mentally disturbed, I don't know which. She can't seem to concentrate. And she's more concerned for her husband than her son. She keeps saying she needs her husband home. Over and over again—she needs her husband home. She has a ten-year-old daughter, Alvo's little half sister, but the girl might as well be invisible for all the notice her mother pays her."

"What about the neighbors?"

"The Jacksons kept pretty much to themselves. They never made the slightest push to get to know their neighbors. The people next door said they've heard a lot of loud arguments coming from the Jackson apartment, but that's about it. None of them like Alvo, and you can't really blame them. He has an attitude guaranteed to put your back up." He leaned his head back against the door. "The boy's scared, Whit. I can see it in his eyes. But I can't get him to tell me what the hell is going on."

After a moment he straightened his back. "That's enough of that. I know I'm becoming obsessed with this case, but I didn't mean to pass it on to you."

She shrugged. "If you can't dump on your friends, what good are they?"

Whitney knew what she had to do now. She had done it often enough. It was her job to entertain him, to distract him so that he could distance himself from his work, if only for a little while.

"Oh my goodness. I forgot to tell you about last night's charity gala," she said with a small laugh. "I can't believe I forgot. I even made notes so I would remember the good parts."

He smiled. "What did you do? You haven't been disgracing the Harcourt name again, have you?"

"It wasn't me this time. It was Baby."

Whitney's cousin, Baby, was full-figured, empty-headed and too close to thirty for comfort. According to Baby, when one reached thirty, it was time to throw out the A list and grab what was available.

"Uncle Ames took one look at the latest and, like Jack's giant, smelled the blood of a commoner," Whitney explained. "He sent Baby on an errand, backed the poor man into a corner and grilled him unmercifully. It turns out that Baby's new man hasn't always been rich. Apparently he made his fortune—a very large fortune by the way—in portable toilets. There's gold in them there privies."

When Dean started to grin, Whitney relaxed and really got into the story, giving the reactions of various members of the Harcourt family to the distressing news. Baby's mother, a woman who prided herself on her control, had almost lost it, right in the middle of the crème de la crème.

"Aunt Jocelyn's face turned purple. I swear, Dean, *purple,* and with that yellow dress, too." She shook her head ruefully. "She was holding onto Uncle Ames like he was a piece of driftwood and she was about to go down for the third time."

It was when her aunt Jocelyn's velvet bowl began to slip down on her forehead that Whitney had noticed a gossip columnist from a local paper standing behind a potted palm, frantically taking notes.

"And that's when I just about lost it myself," she told him with an unrepentant giggle.

By the time Whitney finished relating the story of the infamous Portopotty Incident, Dean was chuckling openly, and the lines of strain had left his face. The tired, worried look was gone from his eyes, and the deep grooves in his forehead had disappeared.

Staring at him, she felt like a traitor for even thinking of reminding him of his work, but she had just thought of something concerning the Gutierrez case.

"Has anyone talked to the little girl?" she said without preface.

And being Dean, he knew immediately what she was talking about. "Sure," he said. "The police questioned her and so did I. Her mother says she was hiding under the bed when the fight took place, and the girl has confirmed that. She says she didn't see anything."

"But no one has talked to her alone, without her mother present?"

He shot a questioning look at her. "You think that would make a difference?"

She shrugged. "I don't know, probably not, but..." She hesitated, reluctant to bring up unpleasant memories. "Dean, would you have said anything bad about your stepfather while your mother was around?"

He stared at her for a long time, frowning. But the frown wasn't from displeasure. It was more as if he was suddenly absorbed in his own thoughts.

Seconds later he rose abruptly to his feet. "You might be on to something, Whit. By God, you just might be on to something."

Without another word, he opened the door and went into the house.

He probably didn't even remember that she was there, she thought with a wry smile. But Dean's neglect didn't really bother her, he was always intense when concentrating on a case. He was just that kind of man. Her kind of man.

Rising to her feet, Whitney moved across the yard, and, after giving the sleeping dog one last pat, she went through the back gate to the alley.

The narrow lane was as clean and orderly as the houses were. All of the plastic garbage cans were color-coordinated and neatly aligned; and flowering bushes peeked cheerfully over the top of well-kept wooden fences.

Most of the houses on Macon Street were 1920's models that young, upwardly mobile couples had bought and restored to their former glory, but the street hadn't always been such a pleasant place to live. When Whitney was six, she'd thought that the street, and the people who lived on it, were somehow different from real people. Like creatures from another world, she found them to be both exciting and scary. Mostly scary. Everyone except Dean. Even back then, when he was well on his way to becoming a juvenile delinquent, Dean had been her hero. And Whitney had badly needed a hero.

When Lloyd Grant died in a boating accident, Whitney had lost more than a father. She had lost her friends and her home, as well, because only weeks after her father's death, she and her mother had left Winnetka, Illinois, and moved to San Antonio.

Anne Harcourt Grant had family in San Antonio. Lots and lots of family. Rumor had it that the Harcourts had been in the Alamo city since Moses was a boy. They were an institution in south central Texas. They were old money. It didn't matter that the fortune Great-great-grandfather Harcourt had acquired before the turn of the century had been made in a real estate scam. Time had obscured the origin of the Harcourt fortune, and each succeeding generation of the family had not only added to the coffers, but had carefully put down another layer of varnish over the self-assumed Harcourt esteem.

Ames Harcourt, Whitney's maternal uncle and the present head of the family, didn't actually work, but he hired people who did, people who invested and acquired. To Whitney, turning a large amount of money into an enormous amount of money didn't seem a worthwhile goal, but it apparently gave Uncle Ames a good deal of satisfaction.

On returning to the bosom of the family, Anne and Whitney had taken possession of a graceful little two-story cottage at the back of the Harcourt's thirty-acre estate. The cottage had been built for Grandmother Harcourt, Whitney's great-grandmother, who had spent her last twenty years there. Uncle Ames called it the Dower House, a pretentious title from a pretentious man. Luckily for Whitney, the cottage sat on the back edge of the property, almost a quarter mile from the main house and Uncle Ames.

When she first arrived in San Antonio, five-year-old Whitney knew nothing of Harcourt history. She had only known that she and her mother were going to be with family. And although her father's death had knocked the wind out of her, she comforted herself with the thought of having cousins to play with, children who would be more than friends because they were blood.

It didn't take he long to discover her mistake.

Whitney had five new cousins. Uncle Ames had two girls and a boy—Allie, Baby and Ames Junior—and Aunt CeeCee, Anne's older sister, had a boy and a girl—Tad and Muffy. Whitney could have gotten used to the ridiculous names, but their attitude was something else. For some reason, all her cousins hated Whitney on sight.

With the exception of Uncle Ames's infant son, her cousins were all older than Whitney, but they went to the same private school that she did; they even had the same riding instructor and the same dance teacher. By all rights, that should have given them something in common. But somehow, from the very beginning, Whitney was out of step.

The Harcourt cousins didn't hesitate to show Whitney that they noticed the difference and were offended by it. They played spiteful little tricks on her when the adults weren't looking. Sometimes the tricks were harmless—like tying knots in the ribbon straps of her ballet slippers, or telling nasty things about her in whispers to the other children at school—but sometimes the tricks were more serious, like the time one of them put a burr under her horse's saddle.

The day it all changed, the day she learned how to get along with her cousins, came almost a year after she and her mother had moved to Texas.

On a muggy summer day, after their shared riding lesson, her cousins began teasing her, the way they always did. But this time a challenge had been issued, and a challenge had been accepted.

To prove she wasn't a sissy-baby, Whitney was to go through the hedge that surrounded the Harcourt estate and bring back proof that she had gone all the way to Macon Street, in the middle of a section of houses that her cousins called "Trash Town."

Ignoring her cousins' jeers, Whitney crawled under the hedge and marched away from them.

It wasn't until she had passed a couple of streets that she realized what she had gotten herself into. During the two-block walk, Whitney had come to understand just why they had called it Trash Town. Rubbish was everywhere, and everything was broken— broken cars in the driveways, broken toys in the yards, broken furniture on the porches. Even the streets were broken. And it suddenly occurred to Whitney that if she stayed there, she might get broken, too.

There was no one to help her. The people she had passed on the street stared at her. And without exception, they all had tight, mean looks on their faces.

So she sat down on the curb and did what she would never have done in front of her cousins. She hid her face between her knees and cried.

"What are you sniveling about, kid?"

Wiping her eyes with the backs of her hands, she looked up. The person standing beside her looked like a man, but was probably little older than Tad. His skin was tanned a deep copper, and his dark hair was long and unkempt, with features that were strong in his thin face. And he had the same anger in his eyes that she had seen in the other residents of Trash Town.

Staring up at him, Whitney stopped crying and swallowed several times in nervous reaction.

"What are you doing in Trash Town?" the boy snarled at her, the anger blazing even hotter in his dark eyes.

"I live here," she lied. "Down that way." She pointed vaguely in a direction. Rising to her feet, she added, "I'm going back home now. It was nice meeting you. Goodbye."

She had begun to walk away when the sound of his laughter stopped her. She turned back to look at him and was instantly captivated by his laughing face.

"Sure you live here," he said, still laughing. "Everybody in Trash Town wears riding pants. Now give. What're you doing here?"

The question made her remember her predicament. She drew in a shuddering breath and sat down on the curb again. Leaning forward, she rested her chin against her fists and sniffed a couple of times.

The boy sat beside her, and after a moment he put his arm around her shoulders. "Come on, kid. What's the problem?"

"Do you know Tad Harcourt?"

"Sure," he said immediately. "Me and Tad, we're just like this." He held up a pair of crossed fingers.

The words made it sound as if he was teasing, but his voice had grown hard again. She studied his face. "You don't like him, either? He's my cousin."

"Bummer," he said in sympathy, then an instant later he whistled softly through his teeth. "You're a Harcourt?"

"Yes... bummer," she echoed mournfully. "At least, Uncle Ames says I am, but I don't know why I have to be a Harcourt when my name is Grant. It says so on my birth certificate. Whitney Daryn Grant. If my Daddy hadn't got drowned I could still be a Grant and live in Winnetka, but he did. Sometimes I cry, but not in front of Tad. The Daryn part of my name is from my father's mother. She's dead, too, but she was probably real sweet. The Harcourts are mostly mean. 'Specially Tad. He hates Amesy... that's Uncle Ames and Aunt Jocelyn's little baby. Tad *hates* a little baby. And just because he wanted to be the only boy. I think that stinks. Baby, now, she's not too mean. She's mostly just dumb. But the others are great big snots. Allie calls me Spitney and Muffy says I have cow eyes and I don't think she's ever seen a cow, because their eyes are brown and mine are blue. I like our house, but you know what? I don't call it Dower House like the others do. Don't you think that sounds like it would make your mouth pucker if you took a bite? I call it Sweet House because it's the sweetest house, and I—"

"Quiet!"

She stopped talking and looked at him, not in the least offended.

"Do you always talk so much?" he asked warily.

"Yes," she admitted, "but it's mostly to myself. Mother is always busy with something else, and I wouldn't talk to my cousins for anything. I mean not like I'm talking to you. I have to talk to them at—"

"I get the picture," he said, interrupting her again. "But what does all that stuff have to do with you being over here in Trash Town?"

She studied his face. "It's an ugly name. I wouldn't call it that if *I* lived here. Don't you mind people calling your home something ugly?"

Apparently it was the wrong thing to say, because the mean look came into his eyes again. "Are you gonna tell me why you're here or not?"

She gave a heavy sigh. "Tad and the girls said if I'm not a sissy then I have to bring back proof that I've been all the way to Macon Street." She glanced around, then back to him. "Do you know which one is Macon Street? I can't find any street signs."

He stared at her for a moment, his expression reflective, then he stood up. "Come on," he said abruptly.

Without hesitation, Whitney followed him. They walked down a dirty, weed-infested alley and presently stepped across what had once been a chain-link fence, entering a yard filled with knee-high grass.

"Stay here," he said as he jumped and caught a low limb on a huge oak tree.

"Wait," she whispered urgently as he began to disappear into the leaves. "Whose house is this?"

"Mine," he said without looking back.

"Then why can't you use the door?"

"Because my stepfather got laid off again," he called back to her. "If I go through the house, he'll pick a fight, and I'm not in the mood today."

Whitney could certainly understand that. She felt the same way about her cousins.

"Wait," she said again as he began to move. "You didn't tell me your name."

"Dean . . . Dean Russell. Now will you pipe down and let me take care of business?"

She watched him climb in through a second-story window, then she stood quietly waiting for him to return. Seconds later he dropped out of the tree and landed a foot away from her. Pulling a battered street sign out of his shirt, he handed it to her. She turned it over gingerly. Macon Street.

"I ripped it off a couple of weeks ago," he said.

"You mean . . . you mean you're *giving* it to me?" she asked, surprise and pleasure making her voice squeak.

He shrugged his thin shoulders. "You need it more than I do. Besides I can get all the street signs I want."

Although he was making light of the gesture, Whitney knew he had given up a great treasure, and she couldn't thank him enough. She thanked him until he told her to shut up again.

"What do you do when they start raggin' you?" Dean asked as they walked back through the streets of Trash Town.

"I punch them," she said, swinging her fist at the air to give him a sample of her right hook.

"Well, that's where you make your mistake," he told her. "Since they're all bigger than you, you couldn't do 'em much damage, and when you start fighting, you're showing them that they can get to you. I found out a long time ago that you gotta show bullies that nothing they can do bothers you, and they're not nothing but a fly buzzing around your head. If you act like their worst tricks are just a big, stupid joke, they'll get tired of doing it. They'll go find somebody that cries or gets mad. See what I mean?"

Whitney nodded, taking in every word as though he had just come down from the mountain after having a long talk with a burning bush. She would follow his suggestion, she told him as they parted at the fortune-teller's parking lot. And then she would come back to Trash Town and tell him all about it. Because Trash Town no longer frightened her. It was where Dean lived.

That day had been the beginning for them. In the eighteen years that followed, a lot of changes took place. Trash Town no longer existed. The old houses were considered fashionable, and the area was now called West Edge. Dean had gone through college and law school and had become a respected attorney. His stepfather had walked out years ago, and his mother lived with her sister in Florida.

As for the advice Dean had given her on that first day, it had worked, and eventually a truce had been called among the Harcourt children. Whitney's cousins had mellowed with age, and sometimes she even found herself almost liking them.

In eighteen years Whitney had grown from a little girl to a woman. She had been through six years of college and was on her way to becoming an expert in her field. And in all that time Dean, in her mind, had never once stopped being her hero. She still went to him when she was in trouble or when she had a triumph to share. And he was always there for her.

Of course she was in love with him. How could she not be? But to Dean, Whitney was still just a little girl he had rescued on that day so long ago. Maybe she always would be.

Chapter Two

"You want to tell me why you're out here digging holes in my backyard?"

From her stooped position Whitney glanced over her shoulder. Dean stood at the back door with a cup of coffee in his hand. He wore only jeans. No shirt, no shoes. He hadn't even combed his hair yet.

"I'm digging for buried treasure," she said. "Inca gold ... Marie Antoinette's jewels. Yeah, that's it."

"You're too late." He walked down the steps and moved to stand beside her. "I hocked all that stuff last week."

It was Saturday, more than a week since she'd brought Oscar to him. And, as Dean had predicted, the Watkins boy had taken one look at the disreputable animal and fallen in love. Pete Watkins had shown more resistance to Oscar's charms, but eventually Dean had talked him into giving the dog a home.

"I brought you some flowers—" she held up a plastic pot "—to brighten up your backyard. It's a thank-you for rescuing Oscar. Aren't they pretty? I bought some just like them for the garden behind Sweet House."

He frowned. "I thought I told you to stop buying me things."

"I'm not trying to corrupt you with ill-gotten Harcourt booty," she said. "I used money gained from the honest sweat of my very own brow." She grinned up at him. "I baby-sat with Allie's three darlings, ill-gotten Harcourts all."

"Then I thank you sincerely." He rubbed the top of his chest, and then, as if he suddenly realized he wasn't dressed, said, "I'll be right back."

Minutes later he reappeared, this time fully dressed his hair neatly combed.

Pity, she thought with a wistful little sigh as she turned back to the flowers.

"It looks like you bought out the nursery," he said, squatting beside her. "What have you got here?"

"A little bit of everything—impatiens, pansies, begonias. And these are caladiums. They'll look good against the house. You should have seen the plants the man at the nursery tried to sell me first. Pale, sickly things. The poor plants were practically coughing."

"Camellias?" he suggested.

"Smart aleck," she said, laughing. "You wouldn't have thought it was so funny if you'd got stuck with a backyard full of consumptive plants. Which is why I badgered him until he took me into the back where all the top-drawer plants live."

"Better neighborhood in the back?"

"Indubitably."

Chuckling, Dean stared at her bent head. There were times, like now, when she was playing the clown, that Dean found himself suddenly taken aback by her beauty. She took her looks so completely for granted—the rich black hair that fell across her face as she worked, the complexion that was like antique porcelain, and the eyes that were bluer than ordinary eyes had a right to be—that he found himself taking them for granted, as well. Then the light would hit her at just the right angle, or she would move her head in a certain way, and the sight of her would take his breath away.

In the past few years, Whitney's body had filled out. Beautifully. She was still slender, her curves not the conspicuous kind, but she had legs that went on forever, and there was something about the way she moved that exuded vitality and subtle, energetic sensuality.

Or maybe it was only subtle to him, he thought ruefully. More than once, the sight of her walking down a street had sent construction workers into a howling frenzy.

Although Dean had always treated Whitney with casual indulgence, there was nothing casual about his feelings where she was concerned. He had been worrying about her for most of his life. He still worried about her, because, even though she was an adult, he couldn't stop thinking of her as fragile. She was a Harcourt orchid raised in an artificial Harcourt environment, an upbringing that had left her ill-equipped to deal with the harsh atmosphere of the real world.

Maybe it would have been different if Whitney hadn't lost her father. From what she had told him, Lloyd Grant had been the exact opposite of his wife. He had been a man with both feet planted firmly on the ground, a man who would have made sure his daughter knew how to deal with reality.

When Dean first met Whitney she had talked about her father constantly, telling Dean about all the things they had done together and how much she missed him. Although she didn't talk about him so much anymore, Dean knew that, even now, she felt his absence in a million little ways.

But Lloyd Grant had died, and although Dean had done his best to provide a masculine influence in Whitney's life, it wasn't the same. His presence in Whitney's life had been a secondary thing, too equivocal to count for much. She had always needed—still needed—stability. She needed the strong, solid grounding of her father to neutralize the Harcourt influence.

"How's the case going?"

He glanced up, startled for a moment, and realized she was studying his face. Picking up another of the potted plants, he shook his head. "Nothing new yet.

I walked Tess—she's Alvo's little sister—home from school yesterday, and I'm almost sure you're right about her, that she's holding something back, but she still isn't talking. She doesn't trust me.''

"She will.'' Whitney smiled. "You have a way of getting right into the heart of a little girl." She took the pot from him and turned it upside down to dislodge a lush caladium, then she looked up and caught his eye. "Guess what? I may have a job for the summer."

"Don't tell me. The nursery man took one look at you and said, 'By golly, I like a girl with spunk. Come work for me and nurse my gasping gardenias back to health.' ''

She tossed her head haughtily. "I don't doubt he was thinking exactly that, but the job I'm talking about is with Boedecker and Kraus."

"The copier people?" He frowned. "What do you know about copiers?"

"Nothing," she admitted readily. "But the Japanese who bought them need an apprentice art buyer. By a strange coincidence I happen to have a degree in Art History. If I get the job, I'll be flying all over creation this summer... maybe even to Europe. Sounds good, huh?"

"It sounds great," he said slowly. "When will you know for sure?"

"I have an interview on Monday. But I can't remember what time— Don't roll your eyes at me like that. It wasn't my fault. The secretary set a time, then changed her mind. But I'm almost sure it's either at ten, ten-thirty, or three."

Dean laughed, finding her brand of emphatic ambiguity as irresistible as always. It was, however, another example of the distance that separated Whitney from the rest of the ordinary world.

The first time Dean had gone out on a job interview he had been a nervous wreck for a week before. And then he'd showed up an hour and a half early to make sure he would be on time—that was the way it worked with most people. But Whitney wasn't most people. She was a Harcourt and therefore had never tasted the bitterness of defeat. She didn't even realize it was a possibility.

She would most likely get the job. Whitney could charm an enraged bull out of its horns if she set her mind to it. But he was having a hard time picturing her in a fast-paced, nerve-racking, corporate atmosphere. She was too naive and, at times, too emotionally immature.

Whitney had never held a job in her life, and suddenly she was going to be flying all over the world on business trips? The very idea scared him silly.

"Do you really want this job?" he asked, trying to keep his voice casual.

"Of course I do. It will allow me to use what I've learned at school." She paused and turned an audacious look in his direction. "Besides, I already have my wardrobe picked out. I'm going to be the best dressed art buyer in the history of western civilization."

Although Dean laughed along with her, he was still uneasy. Her news shouldn't have affected him this way. He had been pushing her to spread her wings, to find a life of her own, since she was eighteen. But somehow he'd thought that whenever she got around to it, it would be a more gradual change. He'd figured she would ease her way into a more well-rounded life.

He should have known better. Whitney never did anything halfheartedly. With her it was all or nothing.

When they finished with the last plant, he stood up and dusted off the knees of his Levi's. "The flowers are beautiful, Whitney. Thanks for thinking of them."

She rose to her feet and glanced around. "They do make the backyard look nice, don't they? They bring a little sparkle to your austere domain. Like Mother always says, 'Accessorize, Whitney, accessor—'"

Before she could finish, he wrapped an arm around her neck and brought her head down so he could rub his knuckles across the top.

"You're bad," he said, chuckling as he released her. "Now make yourself scarce. I have a lunch date and I should probably scrape off some of this dirt before I leave."

"Business?" Whitney asked hopefully.

"Pleasure," he corrected.

She made a face. "Barbara Charles again? Are you sure she's a trustworthy sort of person? I think I remember seeing her picture up at the post office . . . no, listen," she said when he burst out laughing. "Really, I could have sworn it was her. Her hair was stringier in the picture, but she has the kind of hair that would do that if it wasn't washed often enough. Not that I'm implying Barbara isn't a *clean* person, but— Would you stop laughing? I just don't happen to think she's right for you. She seems to be a cold, calculating sort of woman."

Whitney abruptly glanced at him. "She *is* cold, isn't she?" she asked with fading optimism.

"No, she isn't," he said flatly. Taking her arm, he walked her to the back gate. "Now get out of here." Pushing her out, he closed the gate firmly behind her.

"Dean?" she called out, standing on her tiptoes even though the fence was six feet high and she couldn't possibly see over it. "Dean, listen. I wasn't going to mention this, but Barbara's a lot older than you think she is. Modern makeup can work miracles, but I promise you, when she takes it off, her face is going to look like an aerial view of the Dakota Badlands."

When she only heard more laughter from the other side of the fence, she kicked one of his plastic garbage cans and muttered, "The woman has fat ankles. Of course, she might simply have been retaining water on the day I met her," she allowed generously.

"Okay," she said, raising her voice again, "I'll admit it…I'm jealous. If you go out with her it will hurt my feelings. You don't want to hurt my feelings, do you, Dean? *Dean?*"

The sound of his laughter faded and seconds later she heard his back door close.

Exhaling a resigned sigh, she turned and walked down the alley. She was going to have to walk all the way around the block to the front of his house to pick up her car. He probably hadn't stopped to consider how she had managed to get the plants to his house this morning. He probably thought she had twitched her nose and magically transported half a nursery to his backyard. Or maybe he thought the Harcourt butler had carried them over for her.

Oh well, a walk would do her good, she decided as the natural buoyancy began to return to her steps. She knew Dean didn't take her jealousy seriously—he didn't take *her* seriously. But he would, she vowed. Someday he would.

When Whitney walked into her home minutes later, her mother was coming down the stairs. Anne Grant was in her late forties, but she had the kind of soft good looks that stayed the same no matter what her age. Beigy-blond hair, beigy-cream complexion. And she always wore flowing pastels. Blurry. Insubstantial. Nothing about Anne Grant was strong, not even her emotions.

Whitney loved her mother, but in all the years she had known her, she had found nothing solid about Anne. No center, no shell. Fluffy was the word that came to mind most often. Fluffy looks and fluffy personality. If you tried to grab her, she would slip right through your fingers, leaving you with only a handful of air.

As Whitney watched her mother, she thought how strange it was that two people could look at the same thing and see something different. When Dean looked at Anne Grant, he saw deluxe, top-of-the-line chocolate with a solid steel center. He said she was smooth and melty on the outside, but that inside there was a core of inflexibility.

Whitney had never been able to see Dean's version of Anne Grant. Her mother just wasn't that strong. In everything, even in minor decisions, she deferred to her older brother. Whitney had no doubt that if Uncle Ames decided to spray-paint Sweet House purple, Anne would simply smile and say that her brother knew what was best.

Anne reacted with equal fluttery confusion to a spot on the carpet as she did to a world disaster, and Whitney couldn't recall ever having had a serious conversation with her. But maybe that was partly her own fault, since she had decided, a long time ago, that striking up an in-depth conversation with her mother would be a waste of time, a little like trying to discuss philosophy with a Boston fern.

When the older woman reached the landing, she finally spotted Whitney.

"But if they didn't have the fabric I ordered, why didn't they call me?" Anne asked. A frown worried her soft features for a moment then drifted away. "It's such a simple thing really. Nothing more than ordinary courtesy. I suppose I'll have to talk to your uncle about this."

"Uncle Ames will straighten them out," Whitney said, her voice sympathetic. She had had years of practice at picking up nonexistent conversations.

"There's no need for you to worry about it anymore. And next time you can go to someone more reliable."

"Well, I will," Anne assured her. "There is simply no excuse for— I'm sorry you missed Madelaine's visit. And of course, she noticed. She'll tell everyone you weren't here and imply that you're careless or that we've argued. I told her that you would have been here if something important hadn't come up, that I was almost sure it was charity work. And it wasn't your fault that I couldn't remember which charity it was."

"I'm sorry, I forgot Madelaine was coming for brunch today," Whitney said with feigned regret. "I was with Dean."

Anne blinked twice and her features stiffened. "Because you're involved in so many things," she continued as though Whitney hadn't spoken. "I assured her you wouldn't intentionally miss her visit."

The obsolete rules and outdated restrictions that her mother lived by had, at one time, driven Whitney right up the wall. But then she had come to see that the rules and restrictions were a form of self-protection. The past was a place where definite lines had been drawn. Right was right and wrong was wrong. The secure, unchanging decrees of the past provided a buffer zone that shielded Anne from the uncertain, constantly shifting present.

After a brief pause Whitney leaned forward and kissed her mother's cheek. "Would you like me to send her a note, telling her how truly distressed I am at having missed her?"

Her mother's face brightened. "Madelaine would like that. Only last week she was pointing out the fact that young people, her daughters in particular, don't seem to understand what the phrase 'good breeding' implies. They mistakenly think it's acceptable to substitute a telephone call for a handwritten note."

Whitney laughed. "And this will give you a chance to one-up your dear friend Madelaine? Well, I'm all for that. Consider it done."

Anne began to huff a denial, then once again switched thoughts in midstream. "I don't know what to think about the Japanese, darling. They're very pleasant people, of course, always bowing and making one feel so wonderfully *honored,* but they're so...so—"

"Foreign?" Whitney offered. "And since they're all so polite, how can you tell which of them is truly socially acceptable or not?"

"Exactly," Anne said, relieved that someone had managed to put her thoughts into words.

Whitney laughed again, shaking her head. If she even hinted that Anne was a bigot as well as a snob, her mother would have been genuinely hurt. Socrates may have thought an unexamined life was not worth living, but Anne Grant seemed to have gotten through most of her life with ethics that were not only unexamined, they were unidentifiable, as well.

"I think if you'll check Amy Vanderbilt, you'll find we're accepting the Japanese socially these days," Whitney said as she turned and ran up the stairs to her bedroom.

In the shower and later, as she wrote the promised note, Whitney's thoughts kept drifting back to Dean. He hadn't returned to his house after lunch. She called him at two, then again at three, four and four-thirty.

At six she began calling every five minutes, pushing the recall button on her telephone again and again until ten o'clock, at which point she reluctantly went to bed.

As she lay in bed Whitney worried herself with possibilities. Had he taken his date out to dinner as well as lunch? Or maybe Barbara had cooked dinner for him. She seemed like the kind of woman who would do a sneaky thing like that, showing him what a perfect little homemaker she was. Maybe they were at her house right now. Maybe they were in her bedroom. In her bed.

Whitney rolled over in an abrupt rejection of the depressing thought. Most of the time she managed to keep a positive attitude about her relationship with Dean, looking forward to better days in the future. But sometimes, late at night, as she lay awake watching silver moonlight stream through the white lace curtains, she would be unable to sleep for wanting him so badly.

Whitney knew she had Dean's friendship; it was the most solid thing in her life. But friendship wasn't enough. She wanted total intimacy. Mind, body and spirit. She wanted Dean to love her as much as she loved him.

For comfort, she closed her eyes and imagined what their wedding day would be like, something she did on

a regular basis. Her mother was the only Harcourt
Whitney would allow to share that special day with
her. She wouldn't let her relatives turn her wedding
day into the kind of circus Allie's and Muffy's had
been. The planning for her cousins' weddings had
taken more than a year. There had been trips to Paris
and Milan for wedding dresses and trousseaus, and
both events had been covered by national magazines.

Whitney wasn't about to participate in such asinine
competition. She would marry Dean in a garden wedding, maybe in his backyard now that it had been
softened by the plants she had given him. It wouldn't
be an elaborate ceremony. It would be simple. Real.
And she would pay for it all with her own money. She
had been living on Harcourt money for most of her
life, and if she had learned nothing else, she had
learned that the interest they charged was too high.

She hadn't decided yet what she wanted Dean to
wear. In a tuxedo he was so beautiful he could make a
grown woman cry, but a tuxedo was a little too Har-
courtish. Something less formal would be better. Dean
looked wonderful in black. And brown. And gray,
maroon, blue, and white. He looked wonderful in the
ratty old cutoff Levi's that he wore when he jogged,
and would look even more wonderful in no clothes at
all, but none of that helped her make up her mind
about what he should wear on their wedding day.

Whitney would ask her mother to give her away.
And Dean would have his law partner, Sam Carter, as
his best man. Evie Ladd, Whitney's best friend from

college, would be her maid of honor and Reverend Brown, Dean's pastor, would perform the ceremony.

After the wedding they would go to the mountains for their honeymoon—Dean liked the mountains—New Mexico, or Colorado, she thought, throwing a bare arm up over her head.

Maybe they would get one of those outrageous suites with a heart-shaped bathtub and a heart-shaped bed. That would make them laugh. People should begin their life together with laughter.

On their wedding night they would sit on the ridiculous heart-shaped bed and share champagne and strawberries. Whitney wasn't all that crazy about champagne, but she liked strawberries, and the idea sounded romantic.

She couldn't make up her mind about what she would wear to bed on the first night. Something long and white and flowing would look good with her black hair. On the other hand, she had really good legs and hated to cover them up. Although she agreed with Dorothy Parker that brevity was the soul of lingerie, a skimpy teddy would be too blue-movieish. No, a plain little satin shift would be better, she decided.

Dean would wear silk pajamas. Burgundy silk. But just the bottoms, riding low on his hips, the dark flesh of his lower abdomen exposed, a line of dark hair extending from his navel down to...

Whitney sat up in bed and fanned her flushed face with both hands. After a moment her head fell back against the headboard, and the instant her eyes closed, she saw him again. And again she caught her breath in a rush of pleasure. She not only wanted to see him, she *needed* to see him. She needed to see them together.

There was no silk in her vision now. None on her, none on him. The long, strong line of his body covered hers. Every muscle in his body was strained and tight, and she could almost feel his hot flesh against hers. She could almost feel the hunger in his mouth, in his fingers. She could almost feel his hipbones as he thrust urgently against her softness, her fingers digging into his shoulders and his back, digging into his hard, flexed buttocks.

As she leaned against the headboard in her moon-silvered room, Whitney's fingers actually flexed, as though they were, in reality, touching his warm flesh.

Forcing her eyes open, Whitney drew deep gulps of air into her lungs, fighting for control.

"You're a silly excuse for a woman, Whitney Daryn Grant," she said in a rough whisper. "Really silly, really... *disturbed.*"

Scrambling out of bed, she continued to talk to herself as she fumbled around in the dark for her riding clothes.

"This is a bad sign. A *very* bad sign," she warned as she stepped into formfitting pants. "You know what this means, don't you? It means you're turning into an old maid. Lying alone in your solitary bed, dreaming erotic dreams."

Her next words were muffled as she pulled a cream turtleneck over her head. "The next thing you know you'll be wearing those pitiful little saucer-shaped hats and immaculate white gloves, sharing a house with twenty-seven cats and checking under the bed every night before you go to sleep...just in case there's a man hiding there,'' she said through clenched teeth while struggling to pull on her riding boots.

She managed to get out of the house without disturbing her mother, then walked the quarter mile to the stables, tying the scarf she'd brought along on her head. She had stopped talking to herself, but when she reached Heracles' stall, she talked to the horse as she saddled him, meaningless words that made her feel less alone. In response, Heracles nickered softly against her back to let her know that he sensed the wildness in her and was looking forward to the ride.

In the stable yard, Whitney guided the horse to the mounting block and swung into the saddle. Then, leaning forward, she patted his neck and said, "Okay, boy, let's do it.''

Open pasture lay beyond the mansion of Harcourt House, and as she walked Heracles past the tennis court and the pool, the sound of the horse's hooves on the flagstone terrace was like claps of thunder. Uncle Ames was a light sleeper and would probably hear, which meant he would be complaining to her mother tomorrow—again—but she was in too much of a hurry to worry about him.

As soon as they had gotten far enough, Whitney urged the horse into a gallop, letting him have his head through familiar trees and shrubs that dotted and cultivated part of the estate. Then suddenly open land was before her, and she was free of Harcourt influence.

She rode hard and fast through the fields, feeling the powerful animal beneath her as they both worked off restless energy. Excitement sent her blood racing, and she laughed in pure joy when the wind tore the scarf from her hair.

Half an hour later they topped a small rise. Pulling Heracles to a halt, she stood in the saddle. Below she could see Harcourt House and her own little Sweet House. And beyond that she saw what used to be Trash Town. From her vantage point she could also just make out the top of Dean's house.

It wasn't the first time she had sat on this hill watching his house. In fact, she had given him an antique weather vane so that she could spot his house instantly. This little knoll was the destination of all her midnight rides. Seeing his house, even from a distance, made her somehow feel closer to him. And no matter what was going on in her life, just knowing that he existed, knowing that Dean was in the same world, comforted her.

Before she was old enough and bold enough to take midnight rides, Whitney had walked to the little hill. Sometimes to daydream. Sometimes to brood.

She'd been almost eight when she'd found out that Dean's stepfather was beating him on a regular basis.

The first time she'd noticed the bruises, Dean had shrugged them off, telling her that street-fighting was a way of life in Trash Town. She hadn't liked it, but her faith in Dean was total. If he thought the fights were necessary, she would try not to be upset when she saw his battered face.

But one day she had learned the truth. That day, she had sneaked through the gap in the hedge at home and had run through Trash Town to find Dean so she could tell him about the perfect score she had gotten on a spelling test.

She was still more than a block away from Dean's house when she saw him. He was standing on Adam Street talking to a slightly overweight, balding man.

The anger on Dean's face stopped Whitney in her tracks, and she hid behind a broken baby buggy so she could listen to what was being said without being spotted by him.

"I want to help you, Dean," the man was saying, "but I can't do a thing until you tell me what's going on. Other people have told me, but I need for you to confirm it. Just say it. Say, 'My old man is beating the hell out of me.' That's all you have to do. I can take it from there. I can get some help for you."

"Like what?" Dean asked, his voice sullen. "You gonna turn me over to the social workers so I end up in juvie hall?" He snorted in disgust. "Like I really need that."

The man was silent for a moment. "You know what I'm most afraid of? I'm afraid that one day you'll have had enough and will lose your temper...and wind up killing him. You've got a good brain, kid. Most of the time you don't use it, but it's there, and I don't want to see it wasted in prison. At least let me talk to your mother about this."

Dean moved closer to face the man his features stiff with rage. "You stay away from my mother," he warned. "You hear me? Stay away from her. If it's like you said—and I'm not admitting nothing—even if my stepfather is doing what you think he's doing, what do you think it's like for her? Do you think she'd be safe with me gone?"

It took a while, but the truth had finally dawned on Whitney. She didn't take in the rest of what was being said, because the blood was pounding too loudly in her ears.

Jumping out from beyond her hiding place, she started to run. She was running from words she didn't want to hear. She was running from reality.

She hadn't gone more than half a block when arms came around her from behind, holding her twisting, struggling body tight.

"Whit—Whit— For pete's sake, would you stop kicking me?"

She looked up at Dean, but after a moment she began to struggle again. "Let me *go!*" she ordered hoarsely.

"Why? What are you doing here? Where are you going in such an all-fired hurry?"

She gulped air into her burning lungs, and without looking at him, she said in a tight whisper, "Uncle Ames has guns. There's a room in Harcourt House that has guns everywhere, on the walls and in cabinets. I'm going to get one, and I'm going to shoot him."

Dean was quick. He always knew what she was thinking, sometimes even before she knew. He pulled her down to sit on the curb, his arm around her holding her still.

"I wish you hadn't heard any of that," he said, and he sounded angry again.

"Well, I did. You shouldn't have lied to me, but I don't care about that now. Alls I care about is—"

"Getting a gun to shoot him," he said with a strange combination of sorrow and amusement. "You're not going to shoot anyone. And if I catch you anywhere near your uncle's guns, I'll beat your butt. You hear me?"

She sagged. "Dean—" She broke off, and dropping her head to her knees, she began to cry, letting the outrage and frustration and anguish come out in her tears.

"Come on, don't do that, Whit," he said, his voice gruff.

She shook her head. "You should have told me. I can't stand it. I just can't stand it. You said you were fighting with other boys and I didn't like it because your poor face got hurt, and I knew you were a better fighter than anyone else and they probably looked a lot worse than you did. But it wasn't boys. It was your own *father* that—"

"Stepfather," he corrected sharply.

"Your stepfather was doing it," she amended. "And he's an adult. He's not supposed to be hurting a kid. They're just not supposed to do that."

He shrugged away her childish logic. "That's life. Stuff happens all the time, even when it's not supposed to. But I want you to stop worrying about it. A coupla times a month he gets fried to the tonsils and he lays into me. Mostly I stay out of his way, but sometimes he catches me. It's no big deal. He's usually too drunk to do much damage." He grinned. "The booze messes up his balance. Come on now. Straighten up your face and tell me why you came to see me."

She wiped her eyes with the back of her hand. "Nothing important. Who was that man you were talking to?"

"My English teacher. He's all right, but he doesn't know much about living in Trash Town."

"I wish you didn't, either," she said fervently. "I wish you could come and live with me in Sweet House. Mother never hits."

He threw back his head and laughed. "I can just see your mother if you brought me home. 'Whitney, dahling, quick, call the bug man. We've been invaded. And for heaven's sake, don't *touch* him.'"

She started to punch him, then she remembered his stepfather and leaned her head against him instead. "Promise me you'll be more careful. Promise me you'll stay out of his way from now on."

He had made the promise, a hand over his heart in a mock-solemn vow, but periodically she would see bruises on his face again. After that first time he wouldn't let her talk about it again. But that didn't stop her from thinking about it, and it didn't keep her from worrying about him. She would sneak out of the house late at night and watch his house, praying that he was safe, asking God to watch out for him.

Even now, years after the fact, it still hurt her to think about the kind of childhood Dean had had. He had been her protector, but there had been no one to protect him, and she found the inequity difficult to swallow. She not only wanted the beatings to stop, she had wanted Dean's stepfather to pay for what he had done. She had wanted the police to take him away and lock him up for the rest of his life.

Dean hadn't killed his stepfather as his English teacher had predicted, but he had gotten big enough and strong enough to make the man think twice about picking a fight.

And eventually Dean's stepfather walked out, leaving before he could get what he deserved. Whitney had never told Dean, but that part still bothered her. Even though she knew the man was an alcoholic and probably lived in his own special brand of hell, it still infuriated her that Dean's stepfather had never been made to pay. Someone should have been held accountable for the theft of Dean's childhood.

"I'll make it up to him," she said to the night. To the stars. To God. "I'll make him happy, I swear I will. When we're married, I'll make sure his life is full enough and happy enough to make up for all the bad."

He might be dating Barbara What's-Her-Face now, he might even be sleeping with her, but someday that would change. Whitney knew that in her heart.

Someday she and Dean would be together. They had to be.

Heracles shifted beneath her slightly, and as she watched, a light came on in the house with the antique weather vane.

She felt her muscles relax and seconds later she stifled a yawn. She could go back to Sweet House now, and this time she would be able to sleep. Dean was home.

Chapter Three

Whitney sat in the front passenger seat of her mother's dove-gray Mercedes. Anne was driving, her white-gloved hands holding the big steering wheel in a death grip.

The sight of her insubstantial mother behind the wheel of a car always struck Whitney as slightly preposterous. It was a little like watching a cartoon character—Mr. Magoo or the little old woman who owned Tweetie Bird—step off the screen into real life.

The fact that Anne's beigy-cream features were obscured by a wide-brimmed, mint-green hat added to the feeling of unreality, but of course Harcourts always wore hats. Whitney's own—navy blue with big white polka dots—matched her gloves and the bow at the neck of her white dress.

Whitney had planned on attending Dean's church today. It was a friendly, comfortable place where people said amen out loud and the music had some spirit to it. But Anne had felt that a show of Harcourt unity was essential on this particular Sunday, so Whitney had found herself going to church with them. All the Harcourts had been present at the regular Harcourt church, nodding with just the right amount of noblesse oblige as the minister thanked Uncle Ames from the pulpit for his generous contribution to the building fund.

"I don't think she was there," Anne said to Whitney as they were driving back to the estate. "I looked for her. Unobtrusively, of course. It's all well and good to say that another individual's opinion of one doesn't really count, but to be accused of slighting a friend *hurts,* darling. I had my mind made up that I would greet her, but *not* fulsomely."

"And then she didn't show up?" Whitney asked. Her voice was sympathetic even though she didn't have a clue as to the identity of the mysterious "she." "That's tough. Such a good plan, too."

"Yes, it's annoying. The minute Madelaine mentioned it, I told myself I couldn't let it slide this time. I said to myself, 'Anne, this has gone on long enough. This time you simply *must* take strong action.'"

Whitney nodded, her expression earnest, her eyes sparkling with amusement. Talking to her mother was a little like a carnival ride. You never knew where the next curve would take you.

"That's exactly how I would expect you to react," Whitney said. "I don't know how often I've said, 'My mother is a woman of action.' And given the circumstances, I can see that extreme measures...like not greeting her with wholehearted enthusiasm—" She broke off and shook her head. "Well, I can only say I admire your courage, Mother. I truly do."

During Whitney's speech the Mercedes had slowed to a crawl, an indication that Anne was in deep thought. It was a curious phenomenon. Whitney had never met another person whose brain was directly attached to her foot. Anne could either think or maintain acceleration. To do both simultaneously was a physical impossibility.

"Perhaps it *was* a bit extreme," her mother said finally.

It was too much. Whitney let out a loud whoop of laughter, which resulted in confusing her mother enough to bring the Mercedes to a full stop.

"Mother...Mother, everyone's honking," Whitney said, choking out the words as she tried to stop laughing. "Mother, they're— They're getting angry."

But the woman of action was too busy sputtering indignant half thoughts to pay attention to the line of cars behind her. When Whitney saw a very large, very red-faced man get out of a pickup, she pushed her mother's foot out of the way with her own and pressed sharply on the gas.

"Whitney... *Whitney!*" her mother said in a squeaky gasp as she began steering frantically.

During the rest of the drive home, even after Whitney had relinquished control of the acceleration pedal, Anne continued to mutter breathy, cryptic remarks. Whitney caught something about an Uncle Ethan who always wore a pink carnation behind his left ear, but apparently, being a Harcourt, he had managed to carry off the thing with dignity. The only other complete thought was Anne's fear that being thrown from a horse when she was eight had somehow damaged Whitney's sensibilities.

"I'm sorry," Whitney said as the two women entered the house together. "I shouldn't tease you... I know I shouldn't tease you." She kissed her mother's flushed cheek. "But it's all your own fault. You're just so adorable when you're flustered."

In an act of contrition, Whitney listened with a straight face to the lecture that followed. Then, after promising to accompany Anne to a luncheon she'd previously planned to avoid with the excuse, if need be, of an emergency appendectomy, Whitney left her mother and went upstairs.

Half an hour later Whitney, changed into denim shorts and a yellow tank top, was in the process of carrying plants from the shed to the little garden behind the house.

Although the black earth beneath her fingers was slightly cold, Whitney didn't notice. She was thinking, as usual, about Dean, wondering if he had slept late this morning, wondering if he had a reason to sleep late. Like physical exhaustion brought on by a night of hot, unrestrained sex.

After apologizing to the pansy she had almost squeezed the life out of, Whitney sat back on the flagstones and wrapped her arms around her bare legs.

She knew Dean had sex with the women he went out with. She had always known. But she also knew that none of the women he had it with were important. None of them was permanent. They were nothing more than mere interludes, episodes of short-term affection. Not one touched the heart of him.

But, she thought with a short laugh, she would have been less than honest if she didn't admit that she would gladly sacrifice a couple of important limbs if he would consider her for the position of his next babe de jour.

After a few minutes of exploring the possibilities, she decided her luck wasn't that good, and she reluctantly turned her attention back to the plants.

Whitney was working on relocating the last begonia when she remembered her interview at Boedecker and Kraus. She had written the time down. Somewhere. She didn't like the idea of calling to check with the secretary; it probably wouldn't give the right impression if she let them know she had already forgotten the time of her appointment. That didn't sound at all efficient, and she was pretty sure professional people were supposed to be efficient. And on time.

Giving the earth around the plant one last loving pat, she carried the tools to the shed and washed her hands before returning to the house.

The small study at the back of the house was decorated in the pastels Anne Grant loved so much. It was a gentle room. Gentle colors on the walls, gentle lines to the furniture, and only gentle books were allowed on the bookshelves.

After probing her memory for a moment Whitney moved to her mother's little Queen Anne desk. She had been sitting at the desk when she confirmed her appointment with the secretary at Boedecker and Kraus. She had written the time on something, she remembered that much. But she hadn't used her mother's little lavender notepad. It was an envelope or a receipt or something like that. And then . . .

"And then" was the problem, she thought as she sat down at the desk. She couldn't remember what came next. Had she left the scrap of paper just lying on the desk? It was a definite possibility, and knowing her mother, the paper had probably been swept into a drawer along with anything else that happened to be on the desktop.

After shuffling through the clutter in the shallow middle drawer, Whitney began on the others.

After half an hour there was only one drawer left. *The* drawer. The one where old scraps of paper went to die. The drawer that held Whitney's grade school report cards, dozens of homemade valentines, five-year-old shopping lists and ten-year-old slips with dental appointment reminders. Amelia Earhart's flight plan was probably somewhere in that drawer.

There was no use in putting it off any longer, she told herself. The drawer from hell would have to be tackled.

Or maybe not, she thought seconds later when she tried to open the drawer. It was either stuck, or someone very small and very strong was holding it shut from the inside.

Taking a deep breath, Whitney tugged at it once, twice, but it still wouldn't move. Frustrated, she braced her left foot against the leg of the desk and pulled at the drawer with all her strength. The maneuver worked. It worked so well that the drawer came completely out of the desk and bounced off her bare shin on its trip to the floor.

Whitney spent the next few seconds hopping around on one foot, squeaking through clenched teeth until the pain began to subside. Then, regaining her seat, she rubbed the injured spot as she stared at the papers scattered all over the study floor, literally hundreds of them, all shapes and sizes, festooning the Persian carpet.

Sliding off the chair, she dropped to her hands and knees and began to scoop up handfuls of the papers. It was only after she had cleared away perhaps half of the mess that she noticed a folded sheet of paper wedged in a crack at the back of the drawer.

Curious, she pulled it free and unfolded it. After a quick glance she knew it wasn't what she was looking for, but when she went to return it to the drawer, something stopped her. Opening it again, she saw that it was the last page of a letter, and at the bottom it was signed "Yours forever, Lloyd."

It must be an old love letter from her father to her mother, she thought, probably written during one of his business trips. Although Whitney knew very well she shouldn't read the letter, words on the page jumped out at her, catching and holding her attention.

"How is Whitney?" her father had written. "It still amazes me that I could have fathered such a child. Even when she was an infant, I knew she would be extraordinary. Bright and beautiful and full of life is my Maid Mary."

Maid Mary. The old nickname pulled up vivid images, making her smile. Lloyd Grant had been a big man. Tall, and broad in the shoulders. And his personality had had the same strength. He had worn a mustache, and she remembered that his hair had been as black as hers, only thicker. He had big, strong hands, hands that were strong enough to make her feel safe, gentle enough to make her feel absolutely loved.

Every night, after her mother had brushed Whitney's hair and made sure her teeth were clean, her father would come to her bedroom to tuck her in. Sometimes, when she was too full of energy to settle down, he would hold her on his lap and read to her from her favorite book, *The Merry Adventures of Robin Hood of Great Renown in Nottinghamshire*. At some point the characters had become Robbing Hood, Maid Mary, Lily John and Fried Duck, who, in her imagination, looked a little like Daffy, only crustier.

It was natural that childhood memories should fade. It was a part of life. But this particular memory had stayed strong because after Lloyd's death, Whitney had played the scene over and over again in her mind. It was a piece of her father that no one could take away from her.

As she stared at the letter, reading the parts that didn't have anything to do with her, Whitney found herself bombarded by a whole catalog of emotions. Although she felt the keen sense of loss she always felt when she thought of her father, there were other things, as well. There were memories of the special bond she and her father had shared. There was guilt for having intruded on her mother's personal life. And finally, there was surprise that her mother could inspire such warm feelings in any man, even one as loving as Lloyd Grant had been.

Whitney had five letters that her father had written to her, letters he had sent to her before she could even read. She kept them in a little wooden box in her top bureau drawer. It had never occurred to her that her mother would also have letters. Now, staring at the page, she thought it was sweet and sad and a little out of character for her mother to have saved the letter all these years.

As she began to refold the page, she glanced down at her father's signature and for the first time noticed the date. Lloyd Grant had always dated his letters below his signature, even on his letters to Whitney. The peculiar thing about this letter was that it was dated eleven years ago, when her father had already been dead for eight years.

After staring at the date for a moment, she gave a soft laugh. Her father must have been talking to someone when he added the date. The same thing happened to Whitney all the time. She would be writing a check and start talking to the salesperson, then distracted, would find she had filled in some outrageous amount. It was nice to know that she took after her father, even in a small way.

Laying the letter gently in the drawer, she began to gather up the bits of paper that were still scattered around the room. She was reaching for the last piece— it had somehow landed under a footstool—when her mother walked into the study.

"Oh…you startled the life out of me," Anne said, then frowned as she spotted the desk drawer. "What are you doing? Oh, no, you haven't donated the desk to charity. I didn't mind when you gave away the aubergine bowl…that is, of course, I *minded,* but one gets over these things. But Great-grandmother Winslow's desk? Really, Whitney, I can't allow—"

"The drawer was stuck," Whitney said hastily. "That's all. It was stuck. I pulled it out, papers scattered, but now I've picked them up. It was all perfectly innocent, I promise you." She laughed. "Great-grandmother's desk is safe."

She reached down and picked up the letter from her father. "But look what I found, Mother. It's a letter from Daddy. It was wedged in the back of the drawer.

It gave me a little shock when I saw the date, but then I realized he must have—''

Before she could complete the sentence, the letter was jerked from her hand. ''You— You have no business looking through my desk!'' her mother said, her voice uncharacteristically loud. ''Do you hear me, Whitney? You have *no right* to go through my things.''

Whitney simply stared in stunned silence. Her mother was shaking with anger, her face flushed as her fingers clenched into a fist around the letter.

''Understand this right now.'' Anne's voice had dropped, but it was hard and tight as she continued. ''I will not tolerate this kind of intrusion. In the future you will stay out of my desk, out of my... my personal things.''

The strength in the older woman's voice had dwindled with the final words and an instant later Anne turned and walked out of the room.

Whitney stood and stared in bewilderment at the empty doorway. She had never, not once in her life, seen her mother lose her temper. It left her feeling oddly displaced, as though she had stepped into Alice's Wonderland where ordinary things were suddenly extraordinary, where nothing did what it was supposed to do. She felt as though she had been bitten by a butterfly.

Later, after Whitney had showered and changed into a blue silk jumpsuit, she curled up in the window seat in her bedroom and stared out the window, a confused frown adding small grooves to her brow.

Even now, after she'd had time to think, the scene with her mother had a surreal quality about it. Every motion and emotion seemed strangely exaggerated and out of place. Why did her mother suddenly object to Whitney using her desk? Menopause was already behind Anne Grant, but could there be some other physical problem, one that her mother was hiding from Whitney?

No, Whitney told herself, it wasn't about the desk. It was the letter. The change in her mother had taken place when Whitney mentioned the letter from her father.

Leaning her forehead against the glass, she replayed the scene in her mind. She had already admitted to herself that she'd been wrong to read the letter. Letters were personal things, especially a letter from a loved one. But the more Whitney thought about it, the less she was inclined to believe her mother's outburst had been sparked by an invasion of her privacy. For one brief moment, as she'd stared at the letter, Anne Grant had looked afraid.

It was only moments later that Whitney saw her mother leave the house and take the path that led to the main house. As she watched the older woman disappear from sight, Whitney chewed on her lip in indecision. Then she stood up abruptly and left her bedroom.

Downstairs, Whitney returned to the study and began once again to search through the drawers of her mother's desk. This time she unfolded every scrap of paper. She looked in every cubbyhole and between the pages of Anne's appointment book.

Whitney wasn't sure what was driving her; she wasn't even sure what she was looking for, but she knew she couldn't stop until she had some answers.

And that was why, when she left the study, she went upstairs to her mother's bedroom.

As she searched through her mother's personal things, in the bureau, the nightstand and the closet, guilt nagged at Whitney, but the guilt wasn't strong enough to overcome her need to know.

She found nothing in her mother's bedroom. Absolutely nothing. No letters, no mementos, no photos. Frowning in frustration, she wandered into the adjoining bathroom, stopping abruptly as the smell of smoke reached her.

It wasn't tobacco smoke—Anne Harcourt Grant would never do anything so unladylike—more of a charred or burned smoke. Something had been burning in the bathroom. And it had been burning recently enough that the smell still lingered in the air.

Whitney found the evidence, still warm, in a brass wastebasket.

Dropping to her knees beside it, she began to sift through the mound of ash, her fingers trembling with a growing sense of urgency.

She found two scraps of paper in the remains. On one, in her father's distinctive hand, were the words "please, love." The other piece was the top half of an envelope with the return address still intact: *1132*

Quintan Street, Dallas, Texas. The postmark showed it had been sent only seven years earlier.

For a long time Whitney sat on the cold tiles of the bathroom floor, staring at the scraps of paper, then she rose slowly to her feet and walked out of the bathroom. By the time she left the house, she was running.

She took the path she had seen her mother take only minutes earlier, stumbling several times as she went. It was when she rounded a decorative evergreen bush that she saw her mother and uncle standing together on a small terrace that extended from the side of the main house.

Whitney stopped running and moved toward Anne Grant with carefully deliberate steps.

"Tell me how Daddy died." Her voice was breathless from exertion, agitated from disbelief. "You never told me any details. Not one. You just said he drowned in a boating accident. When I was little, all I cared about was that he wasn't coming home again, then later, when you never mentioned him, never even spoke his *name,* I just assumed that it was too painful for you to talk about. I *hurt* for you, Mother. You had lost a life partner, and I could see...anyone could see that you weren't strong enough to cope on your own."

She shook her head slowly. "All these years, I thought I had to protect you. I thought you were too vulnerable, too *soft,* to deal with reality. I thought it was my job to do that for you. I honestly believed that's what Daddy would want me to do. You see...you see, I felt—"

She broke off and drew in a deep, steadying breath. "You have to tell me the truth, Mother. You have to tell me *now*."

"Whitney, for heaven's sake," Anne said, her voice flustered. "You're overheated. Look at your face, darling, it's all flushed and—"

"Did my father die nineteen years ago?"

"Whitney, calm down immediately!"

The barked order came from her uncle, but she ignored it as she kept her gaze trained on her mother's face. "Mother, please." Her voice was quieter now, calmer, but none the less determined. "Just tell me the truth. Did Daddy die like you told me he did?"

When Anne glanced away from her, avoiding her eyes, Whitney knew she had stumbled onto the truth. The inconceivable had suddenly become fact.

"All these years," she whispered hoarsely, her voice shaking with anger and anguish. "All these years, you've been *lying* to me. How could you do it? How could you coldly and deliberately tell a five-year-old child that her father was dead? It was cruel. You knew what he meant to me. You *knew*."

Whitney's fingers clenched into fists as rage overwhelmed her. "Every day...*every damn day* for nineteen years I've mourned him. I've *grieved* for him. Every single day I tried to fill up the hole that his death left in me. But it never worked, Mother. The hole couldn't be filled." Her breath was coming in harsh gasps now. "You lied when you said he was dead, and you just kept on lying, no matter how it hurt me. For all my life, you've been telling *one damn lie after another!*"

"That's enough," her uncle said, his voice hard. "Don't you take that tone with your mother."

Instantly Whitney shifted her gaze to him. "You knew, didn't you?" She gave a short, harsh laugh. "Why doesn't that surprise me, Uncle Ames?"

"I did what I thought was best."

The soft, trembling words brought Whitney's gaze back to her mother. Anne's pale hands were clasped to her breast, her gaze on a distant point as she still refused to meet the accusation in her daughter's eyes.

"I did what I had to do," Anne said, nodding her head as though she were responding to a question only she could hear.

"That's no kind of answer," Whitney whispered. "No kind of excuse."

She stared at her mother's face, and it was at that moment that she finally acknowledged the distance between them. But what caused the crippling pain in her chest was that she also realized the distance wasn't something that had sprung up as a result of her accusations. It had always been there. Whitney had no idea who her mother really was. The woman she thought she knew had never existed.

Without another word, Whitney turned and walked away.

Chapter Four

Dean rolled over and looked at the clock, then groaned. It was after one. He had slept half the day away.

When he tried to sit up, he groaned again, louder this time. He felt like death warmed over, and it served him right. He had come home last night and gotten quietly, totally drunk.

Dean rarely drank at all. It always left him with a bad feeling. It always reminded him too much of his stepfather. He had sworn he would never do it, would never use alcohol the way his stepfather had, but occasionally Dean rediscovered the fact that he had learned more than he wanted to learn from the man who had raised him.

This legacy from a man he hated made Dean watch his motives and actions more closely than most people. He was always afraid he would find something else of his stepfather in him. Last night he had definitely seen a resemblance.

Yesterday Dean had taken Barbara to lunch, but he hadn't been able to concentrate on the blonde's cheerful conversation. Barbara Charles was an attractive woman, but not attractive enough, he realized now, to hold his attention for very long. During lunch, his thoughts had kept returning to another woman, a woman with hair like black silk and mischief in her startling blue eyes.

If Dean could have gotten his hands on Whitney, he would have throttled her. Thanks to her comments on Barbara's "police record," every time he looked at his luncheon companion he saw, superimposed over her lovely features, a grainy black-and-white mug shot— both front *and* side views. And then he would start laughing, which hadn't done a lot to endear him to his date. She would probably think twice about going out with him again.

After he had dropped Barbara off at her house, Dean had driven around for a while. Then on the spur of the moment, he'd turned his car in the direction of the apartment building where Alvo lived when he wasn't being detained by the authorities. A little girl had been sitting on the curb, cradling a doll in her thin arms.

Tess.

Dean drove around the block until he found a parking spot, then he got out and walked back to where he had seen Alvo's little half sister.

He didn't say hello to her. He simply sat down beside her. After a while he began to talk, he never addressed her directly, he simply talked. He talked about another little girl he had found sitting on a street curb years earlier. He talked about Whitney, about the times she'd gotten into trouble, the practical jokes she'd played on Dean and on her cousins.

He talked about how different Whitney's life had been from his own, about how she'd lived in a beautiful house and had her very own horse, while Dean had had to sneak into his own house to keep his stepfather from beating him.

It was the first time in a long while that Dean had talked about his stepfather. He wasn't even sure why he had brought it up, but something in the little girl's face told him she wouldn't be shocked. Something told him Tess already knew that bad things happened to children.

It wasn't long before Tess began to ask questions, about Whitney, about Dean. Twilight was settling over the street when the little girl finally told Dean the truth about Alvo's quarrel with her father.

Tess had hidden under the bed—that part of her story had been true—but sounds had still reached her. And she had been present when the fight began.

As though she were talking about a movie she'd seen on television, Tess told him how her father had accused Alvo of stealing two dollars in change from the dresser, how her father had gotten out the rope that he always used to tie up her brother when it was time for another beating.

That was when Tess had left the room to hide under her bed, putting her hands over her ears so she wouldn't hear her father yelling, so she wouldn't hear Alvo crying out in pain. She knew she wouldn't be able to block out all the sounds, but she always tried.

This time, however, was different. This time Alvo rebelled. He refused to be tied up. He refused to be beaten. Tess didn't know what happened next. She didn't know what her brother was doing, but she knew it was bad because she heard her mother screaming for him to stop.

When Tess finally came out from under the bed, medical people were taking care of her father, the police were talking to her mother and Alvo was gone.

Tess's story didn't shock Dean. It made him sad and angry for both children. It made him want to strike out at something, someone, for the children's sake. But it also brought back memories that made him sick to his stomach. For a while, as Tess talked, Dean had become Alvo. He had been thrust forcibly back into the frustration and rage and pain.

But he wouldn't allow the feelings to take control. Not this time. As soon as he left Tess, he went to visit Alvo. And now that Dean was armed with the truth, it didn't take him long to find out that Jackson's threats to kill Alvo's mother and sister had kept the boy quiet.

Dean didn't pull any punches with his young client. He told Alvo that his stepfather wouldn't stay in jail forever. But Dean could make sure that he would stay in long enough for Alvo to get bigger and stronger. He would stay in long enough for Alvo's mother and sister to get psychiatric help. Dean had friends in the district attorney's office. He would make sure Jackson was put away long enough to give Alvo and Tess a chance at a better life.

All in all, Saturday had been a productive day, but after leaving Alvo at the jail, Dean had felt drained of energy and emotion. He'd made his way home, but as soon as he'd walked in the door, ghosts from the past rushed to greet him. He felt the presence of not only his mother and stepfather, but the presence of himself as a boy.

Back then he had been as wild and angry and frightened as Alvo was now. Until he'd found Whitney. Whitney had represented hope. She had shown him that life wasn't all dark, that there were bright spots to look forward to. She had kept him sane. She had kept him from turning on his stepfather the way Alvo had turned on his. As long as Whitney was in Dean's life, there was a reason to push forward, a reason to keep going.

As he'd sat in the empty house, Dean had felt a violent need for Whitney's company. He needed some of her brightness. He needed her to pull him out of the dark hole he'd fallen into. She would help him forget what he had been in the past. She would remind him of who he had become.

He'd almost called her then. He knew she would be beside him in minutes if he did. All he'd had to do was pick up the phone, but he wouldn't let himself do it. This particular hell was his own, and he wouldn't let it touch her. This was a battle he had to fight alone.

And that was when he had taken the first drink. He'd told himself he just needed a couple of drinks to help him sleep. There was nothing wrong with that. But part of him—the logical, objective part—knew what he was doing. He wasn't simply taking a drink to relax. He was confirming that, deep down, he was still that boy from Trash Town. He was still that wild, bad boy who did things decent folk didn't do.

And now, the morning after, Dean was paying for his little excursion into truth. Not only did he have the granddaddy of all headaches, but he felt diminished by his weakness. And he still felt those unbreakable ties with the past.

Pushing back the covers, he slid slowly to the side of the bed. Lying around regretting last night wasn't going to accomplish anything. He had to go see Jackson in the hospital, then start working on getting the charges against his client dropped. Alvo didn't care about Dean's ghosts. He had plenty of his own.

After Dean had it all settled, when his feet were planted more firmly in the present, he would call Whitney and tell her about the case. She would hurt for Alvo and Tess, then she would call him a legal genius and a true humanitarian, he thought with a slight smile. It was the kind of thing he needed to hear today.

* * *

Whitney passed Sweet House and headed for the hedge. When she reached it, she stooped and pushed through the low gap without pausing. She crossed the realtor's parking lot and automatically turned onto Adam Street.

Her father was alive!

Where the hell had truth been for the past twenty years? The question had been playing over and over in her mind, driving her crazy.

Why hadn't she known it was all a lie? Why hadn't she felt her father's presence in the world? Why hadn't she, even once, questioned her mother about Lloyd Grant's death?

But she knew the answer. Whitney hadn't asked questions because she trusted her mother. No matter how flaky Anne Grant was, Whitney had always believed her mother loved her. Until now.

No, she told herself, that part wasn't a lie. Her mother loved her, and Whitney returned that love. Even now. But the ties between them were only those of blood. There would never be—*could* never be—deeper bonds between them. They were too different.

By the time Whitney turned down the alley behind Dean's house she was running again. She needed him now. Just seeing him would show her that not everything about her life was a lie. Dean would help her make sense of it all. Dean would make it stop hurting.

She entered his house through the back door, calling "Dean!", then louder, *"Dean!"*

He wasn't in the kitchen or the office. He wasn't anywhere on the lower floor.

Taking the steps two at a time, she ran up the stairs, down the hall to his bedroom and threw open the door. "Dean, where are—"

It was at that exact moment that Dean stepped out of the bathroom. He was drying his hair with a towel. And he was naked.

The sun streaming through the curtains turned his body to gold, highlighting every muscle, every tendon.

All thought left Whitney's head as they stood and stared at each other. She couldn't take her eyes off him. She had always known he would look incredible without clothes, but nothing in her imagination could have prepared her for the reality.

The energy that, a short time ago, had been wasted in anger and confusion was suddenly channeled into wanting him. Needing him. She had felt a small particle of this urgency before, in dreams. But now, when she could actually see him, when all her emotions were heightened by what she had just learned, it overwhelmed her.

"My God, your body is beautiful," she said in a breathless whisper. "More beautiful than anything I've ever seen."

Across the room, Dean closed his eyes tightly. He had to shut her out. He had to shut out the sight of Whitney looking at him with those hungry blue eyes. He couldn't handle the desire that blazed in her— openly, guilelessly, right there for anyone to see.

Didn't she know that kind of openness could get her hurt?

Whitney didn't know that she had moved until she was a step away from him. She seemed to have no will of her own, and her body was acting of its own accord. She saw her hand move, reach out to him. She felt his chest, warm and damp from the shower, beneath her trembling fingers.

"Beautiful," she repeated, but it didn't sound like her voice. It was lower, huskier. It was shaking with the strength of her desire.

Raising her gaze slowly to his face, she met his eyes. An instant later she jerked her hand away from him and took a step back.

His dark eyes were blazing with anger. Violent anger he was making no attempt to disguise.

He threw the towel savagely on the floor. "Damn you, Whitney!" Reaching around her, he picked up a pair of Levi's and began to pull them on. "What in hell do you think you're doing? When are you going to grow up? For heaven's sake, just *grow up!*" He threw the harsh words at her, his hands shaking as he fastened the jeans. "Don't I have enough on my plate without you pulling these stupid little tricks all the time? Judas priest, I can't turn around without tripping over you."

He pushed a hand through his damp hair. "I have a right to my privacy. Do you understand? You— It's about time you accepted the fact that I have a life of my own, and that I don't have time to play games with a spoiled Harcourt brat." His breathing was ragged now, his lips tight and white. "Get out of here. Just *get the hell out of here!*"

With his first words, Whitney had felt the blood drain from her face, from her heart. She had heard Dean speak in anger before, but never in her wildest imaginings had she ever thought that anger would be turned on her.

Backing away from him, she began to shake her head in denial. She tried to speak, but the words wouldn't come, and when she reached the door, she turned away from him.

"Whitney... *wait!*"

The low, pleading command served to spur her into action. She stumbled on the stairs and had to grab the banister to regain her balance, but she didn't stop. She heard Dean calling her name again and knew he was following her, but that only made her run even faster.

As Dean ran down the stairs after Whitney, he swore under his breath, cursing himself for overreacting. He had to catch her. *He had to make her understand.*

Just as he reached the kitchen the telephone there began to ring, and although he ignored it, it pulled him back to reality long enough for him to stop and think about what he was doing.

He moved to sit at the small wooden table, dropping his head to his hands. He couldn't afford to see Whitney again right now, he told himself. She needed time to calm down, and he needed time to get his act together. Emotions were running too high on both sides and another encounter might be even more disastrous.

He could have handled the whole thing better. He *would* have handled it better if he'd had any warning, but she had taken him by surprise.

The understatement of the year, he thought as he drew in a rough breath.

Dean had always known Whitney had a crush on him, but he had been certain that was all there was to it. A simple little schoolgirl crush. What he'd seen on her face a few minutes ago, however, left that theory in the dust. *That* was more than a crush. Much more. He had seen blazing, blatant desire in her blue eyes. Sweet heaven, he had felt the heat of it, even from across the room.

Whitney wanted him. And when he'd acknowledged that fact, it had taken more strength than he knew he possessed to ignore the wild images her desire conjured up. Images that shocked and tantalized him. Images that took his breath away.

He had been forced to channel the fire she had built in him into fury. It had been necessary for her wellbeing. It had been necessary for his own sanity.

Dean knew very well that if his own feelings hadn't been so strong, he would have handled her differently. He would have dampened the fires in a way that would have left her pride intact. Damn it, he couldn't stand the thought of Whitney in pain. But at the time he had seen no alternative.

Now, after the fact, he realized that he could have turned the whole episode into a joke. Whitney had a keen sense of humor and would have responded to that kind of thing. He could have gentled her over the moment, and when the mood had been broken, he could have eased her into the idea of letting go of him and getting on with her life.

Exhaling a shuddering breath, he told himself that it was too late to change what had happened. It was too late to take back the things he'd said.

He knew Whitney wouldn't hold a grudge against him for what had occurred, for his rash words. That wasn't her style. She would simply find a way to bridge the gap that had suddenly sprung up between them.

And maybe it wasn't such a bad thing after all, he told himself after a while. Hadn't he been trying to ease some distance between them for years now? In the past nothing he'd tried worked. Maybe something more drastic—and the scene in his bedroom definitely qualified as drastic—was needed to start her thinking in the right direction. A direction that, for her own good, had to lead away from Dean.

Leaning his head back against the wall, he reminded himself that Whitney wasn't used to people shouting at her. She had been pampered and protected all her life, but she couldn't stay wrapped up in cotton forever.

It was time for her to wake up and see that the world was a hard place. It was time for her to understand that you have to be tough to survive.

So why did he feel like such a jerk for being the one to push her into reality?

Whitney entered the house through the back door. It was going to be a while before she could look her mother in the face. And now that Dean—

She stopped the thought before it was fully formed, and by the time she reached her bedroom and locked the door behind her, she had successfully pushed the scene in Dean's bedroom out of her mind.

As she sat in the window seat, hugging a cushion close to her chest, she found that her mind was a complete blank. She couldn't feel anything now. Curious. There was no anger, no love, no pain. Very curious.

A fearsome drowsiness took over, and she wasn't sure how much time passed before she heard a knock on her bedroom door.

"Darling... Whitney, your door is locked."

"There's news," she muttered, then sank her teeth into the cushion as bitter laughter rose in her chest and throat.

"Doris Louise Pfeiffer called while you were out. She can't remember if the committee decided on green tablecloths or white. I told her, as firmly as I could without being rude, that you couldn't possibly have voted on green. But you know how she is. Of course I wouldn't say this to anyone other than you, but this is not the first time I've wondered about Doris's taste. When she was only a child, she—"

The laugh was growing out of control, choking Whitney as she buried her face in the cushion. She knew she should thank her mother for providing a distraction. Anne was after all, helping Whitney push the debilitating numbness away.

As energy returned, so, too, did the memory of everything that had happened to her today. Her father, her mother, Dean . . .

No. She still wasn't ready to think about Dean. Someday she would be able to come to grips with what had happened between them, but not now. If she thought about it now, it would kill her.

Drawing in a deep breath, she leaned her head against the cool glass. It certainly had been an interesting day. Her fluffy little mother had finally slipped away from her for good. And just as she had feared, Whitney was left with a handful of nothing. She didn't even have De— Couldn't she even think a single thought without having him intrude? she wondered peevishly. Other things had happened today. Why did Dean keep taking control of her thoughts?

But of course, Whitney knew why. She'd lost him. This was what an earthquake must feel like. This was what it was like when the most solid thing in life shifted beneath your feet. Where did one go, how did one keep standing, when the ground below began to buckle?

Her father was alive, and Dean didn't want her around. Down was up and up was down.

Whitney knew what Anne wanted her to do. Her mother would prefer Whitney pretend nothing had happened. She wanted Whitney to forget that her father, her wonderful loving father, was still alive somewhere in the world.

She moved restlessly on the window seat, finally managing to center her attention on the astounding fact that her father was still alive. Did he know about the lies? Did he know that his daughter thought he was dead? Was he a part of the intolerable deception?

"No," she denied in a hoarse whisper.

He couldn't have known. Lloyd Grant had loved her. There was no doubt in her mind about that. She wouldn't still feel the solid strength of his love after all these years if it had been a lie.

But why hadn't he ever gotten in touch with her? And why had he left in the first place? Even if Anne had driven him away, even if the marriage had gone wrong, why had he disappeared from his daughter's life?

It simply didn't make sense. Nothing made sense anymore, she told herself as she steadfastly ignored her mother, who continued to talk to her through the door.

Fifteen minutes later Anne finally got tired of talking without getting a response and left. Suddenly there was nothing to distract Whitney from her thoughts. There was nothing to keep her from pulling up her stock of memories of her father.

"Where is my Maid Mary going with flowers in her hair?"

"To see the Queen, Daddy. And that's not flowers, it's jewels. You have to wear lots of jewels when you visit the Queen. It's a rule."

"Queen Elizabeth would think you're beautiful, even without flowers."

"Not her, silly. The Queen of Hearts."

"Oh, in that case, you'd better keep the jewels."

*"Mother taught me to curtsy. Do you want to see?
I can do it without falling now. Come with me, Daddy.
You don't have to go to work today. Come with me to
see the Queen."*

For hours Whitney sat in the window seat, unmoving, as silence and darkness spread across her bedroom. It was a little before midnight when she finally stood up and stretched her stiff back.

There were no answers here, she told herself. Not in this room, not in this town. Dean was right. It was time for her to grow up.

It took Whitney nearly an hour to pack and three trips downstairs to transfer all her luggage to her car. She didn't worry about waking her mother—Anne Grant always slept like a log.

Tonight Whitney resented that. She resented the ease with which her mother had blocked out the day's events. Anne should have been up worrying. Guilt and shame should have kept her awake.

But Whitney knew that her mother had already shoved their confrontation into a cubbyhole in her mind, a cubbyhole marked Don't Look. If Whitney stayed here, her mother would never mention it again. It would be as though nothing had ever happened, and maybe, after a while, Whitney would begin to believe that, as well.

She wouldn't let it happen, she told herself as she tossed her makeup case into the back seat of her white Jaguar. She wouldn't turn into a Harcourt and start ignoring what she didn't want to see.

She stood for a moment, looking at the house. During her college years Whitney had lived in a dorm, then in a sorority house, followed by an apartment shared with several friends, but she had always thought of this as home. Not the Harcourt estate, but this house. Sweet House. Here she had been able to watch out for her mother. Here she had been close to Dean.

But the house was just another part of the lies. It wasn't her home, had never been her home. Home was still ahead, she told herself. Home was somewhere in the future.

It shouldn't hurt so much to leave a lie.

Sliding into the driver's seat, Whitney closed the door and started the car, but when she reached the stables, she stopped again, put the car in park and stepped out, staring over the top of the car at the low, dark buildings.

One more time, she thought. One more goodbye. One last midnight ride.

Ten minutes later she was on Heracles' back, headed toward open land. The horse seemed to sense that tonight was different from all the other nights they had ridden together. The wildness and pain that was in Whitney was somehow transmitted to the horse, and they tore across the land as if chased by demons.

Whitney almost laughed when she realized the horse understood her better than her mother did. But she didn't. Instead, she cried. The wind rushed by her, first cooling her tears, then drying them.

When she reached the knoll, Whitney pulled Heracles up sharply. He reared twice, then twitched and snorted, shifting his feet restlessly as though he weren't ready to stop.

"We won't stay long," she murmured, looking out toward West Edge.

Now she would think of Dean.

The lights were still on in his house, and she knew his inability to sleep should have been some small comfort, but the comfort couldn't reach her.

As she sat in the dark, Whitney allowed more memories to wash over her, memories that had nothing to do with her father. Eighteen years' worth of memories.

There were so many pictures of him in her mind. Dean handing her a battered street sign on that first day. Dean roaring with laughter at her outrageous imitation of the first girl Tad brought home to meet the family. Dean carefully explaining how she should behave on a date, telling her openly and frankly about what happened between men and women, something her mother refused to talk about. Dean holding Whitney when she cried.

And finally, after reliving the best of their past together, Whitney knew that what had happened today wouldn't ever cancel any of the good memories.

She wouldn't do as her mother had done and push what she had seen in Dean's face—the anger and contempt—into a Don't Look cubbyhole. It had happened and Whitney would face up to that. Weighed against the love he had given her for eighteen years, it no longer felt quite so devastating.

Almost against her will, Whitney felt better. She felt stronger.

Dean had taught her to use what God had given her. He'd taught her to call upon her inner strength, grab a problem by the throat and wrestle with it until it was resolved. That was what she would do now. She would find her father and get the answers she needed. And when she knew the truth, she would build a new life for herself. She would find a new home.

Reaching down, she patted Heracles' neck. "Okay, boy, I'm ready to leave now." Digging in her heels, she pulled Heracles' head away from the past, toward the future.

Then, turning in the saddle, she gave Dean's house one last long look. "Goodbye, Dean," she whispered. "Take care."

Chapter Five

Whitney pulled to the side of the street, put the Jaguar in park, then spread a street map out on the passenger seat. She had been to Dallas plenty of times, but someone else—a taxi driver or a friend—had always been in the driver's seat. And she was pretty sure she had never been to this part of town. There wasn't a shop or restaurant for miles.

Glancing up, she checked the street sign down the block, then returned her gaze to the map, her fingers moving across the fine lines. She was five blocks from Quintan Street. Five blocks. She was almost there.

The night she left San Antonio, Whitney had thought only of finding her father. Getting her questions answered. Seeing his wonderful face again, and having his arms around her. But now that she had had time to think, doubts were beginning to set in. What if Lloyd Grant had walked out on his family of his own free will? What if he had simply decided he didn't want Anne *or* Whitney anymore.

She had to admit the possibility made sense. Had abandonment been the case, Anne would have been shamed by desertion; she would have been disgraced in the eyes of the world. Her world. Being widowed was eminently more respectable than being dumped.

If Lloyd had left because he no longer loved them, he might not want to be reminded of the family he left behind. He might resent Whitney for intruding. And there was always the chance that he had a new family, one that knew nothing about his old one. Did she have the right to disrupt the lives of innocent people?

Putting the map aside, she closed her eyes and leaned forward, resting her head against the steering wheel. She didn't want anyone to be hurt by her sudden appearance, but neither could she leave without learning the truth.

She would simply have to proceed with care. She wouldn't rush in, telling all and sundry that she was searching for her father. If Lloyd Grant was still at the address on Quintan Street, Whitney would watch and listen until she knew for sure what was going on in his life.

And only then would she decide what to do next, she told herself as she put the Jaguar in gear and pulled away from the curb.

The house at 1132 Quintan Street had a wide porch, supported by pillars that were half brick, half square wooden posts. The tiny yard held a few thin shrubs, but there were no trees, no flowers. It was a no-frills kind of place, and there was an impersonal feel to it. Even before Whitney saw the small faded sign with Rooms printed with a green marker, she knew that this wasn't a private home.

She drove past the house three times before she realized the people on the street were staring at the white Jaguar, and her stupidity made her groan. Of course they were staring. It was a decent neighborhood, clean and uncluttered, but parked in most of the driveways were neat little economy cars or dependable old Chevrolets.

Not a Mercedes or BMW or Jaguar in sight, she thought as she turned the corner and headed back toward her hotel.

Twenty-four hours later, the Jaguar her uncle had given her in her first year at S.M.U. was in storage and Whitney was the proud owner of a '72 Buick.

And that wasn't the only change that had taken place. When she parked the Buick in front of the boarding house and stepped out, Whitney wore faded jeans and an oversized man's work shirt, an ensemble that had always made Anne Grant cringe. Her mother wouldn't see anything funny in the fact that Whitney was finally dressed appropriately.

Her knock on the front door of the boarding house was answered by a gruff-voiced, gruff-faced woman in her late fifties.

"Better come on in," Mrs. Skinner said when Whitney asked about a room. The woman seemed nice but abrupt.

"I don't have any vacancies, but I have a friend who lets rooms, too. Wait here for a minute while I write down the address," she said, already on her way out of the small entrance hall.

"I particularly wanted a room here," Whitney said, panicking for no good reason. When the woman paused, Whitney moistened her lips and added, "You see, this place was recommended by a friend...a friend of my father's. A man named Lloyd Grant."

Mrs. Skinner shook her head, then paused to adjust a hairpin. "No, no one called Grant lives here. There was a man last year. Couldn't stand him, something about the way he was always clearing his throat. What was his name? No, it was Greer. I sure can't remember a Grant." She turned away again. "I'll get that address for you." And she was gone before Whitney could stop her.

"Lloyd ain't lived here for four or five years at least."

Startled, Whitney whirled around and saw an elderly man making his way slowly down the stairs.

"What did you say?" she asked as the blood began to pound in her ears.

"I said old Lloyd hasn't lived here for quite a while now," the man said, speaking loud and slow as though he suspected her of being hard-of-hearing.

Whitney swallowed around the lump in her throat and wiped her damp hands on her jeans. "I wonder—I wonder if it was the same man. His . . . his wife was a tall, dark woman.''

The old man shook his head. "Naw, couldn't have been him. Lloyd was an old bachelor like me. Still is as far as I know. Least, he didn't say anything about a wife when I saw him last month."

"You saw him? Where was that?"

When Whitney saw the old man's features close up, she realized the questions had been too urgent, too sharp.

Softening her lips into a smile, she said, "Maybe I was mistaken about the wife. I mean, I never actually met her. It might be the same man. The thing is, Mr.... You see, I'd really like to get in touch with Mr. Grant."

"What for?"

Oh, yes, he was definitely suspicious, she told herself ruefully.

Perspiration had gathered in her palms again, but as she nervously tangled her hands in the bottom of her shirt, she maintained the smile.

"I—I owe him money," she said, searching desperately for a plausible excuse. Everyone understood about an honorable debt. "He was kind enough to lend me some money several years ago, and now that I'm doing better, I'd like to repay him. Do you know where he's living now?"

He shook his head. "That sounds like Lloyd and I'd sure like to help him out, but he didn't say a word about where he's staying. I ran into him over to Rick's Pub out on Rale Street. I think Lloyd's a regular there, but it's not my kind of place," the old man muttered. "Too noisy. My nephew took me there for a beer. He's young enough to put up with that loud music. Rock and roll, you know. Now, Westler's up town is more my speed. They have good old country music, and all my buddies go there. Especially on—"

"Thank you, sir," Whitney said, already turning to pull the door open. "Would you tell Mrs. Skinner I don't need that address after all and thank her for me?" The last words were thrown over her shoulder.

Whitney's hands were shaking on the steering wheel as she pulled away from the curb. As soon as she was out of sight of the boarding house, as soon as she turned off Quintan Street, she pulled over to the side of the street and slumped forward.

Her father was *still* alive.

Whitney's one big fear, a fear she had hidden somewhere in the back of her mind, was that Lloyd Grant had died since writing those letters to her mother. That she would have to face his death all over again.

But he was still alive. And there was no new family to disrupt. She could find him, making herself known to him, without worrying about the other people in his life.

Tonight she would go to Rick's Pub on Rale Street and start asking— She broke off the thought as another occurred to her. She already accepted the possibility that her father had walked out because he was tired of having a family. But if she started asking questions and word got back to him, he might disappear again.

She couldn't take that chance. Although it went against the grain, she would have to be patient. She wouldn't mention his name to anyone. The old man at the boarding house said Lloyd Grant was a regular at Rick's, so Whitney would also become a regular. She would listen and watch, and sooner or later she would find him.

The decision made, she put the car in gear, waited for a station wagon to pass, then pulled out.

Whitney didn't look forward to going back to the hotel. The room was too empty, too lonely, and she would have to fight herself to keep from calling Dean. She needed to talk to him. And although she wanted to tell him about everything she'd learned, about the detective work she'd done, she knew it would be enough just to hear his voice.

It wouldn't be the first time in the past two days that Whitney had fought the urge to call Dean. She'd said goodbye to him on a hilltop, but she was discovering that goodbye was only a word. And one little word couldn't cancel out the habits of a lifetime. She was in the habit of thinking of him. She was in the habit of sharing her thoughts and feelings with him.

She was in the habit of loving him.

It would get better, she told herself. It had to. As soon as she found her father, she wouldn't feel so alone. She would have something other than Dean to think about.

And someday she would probably get used to the pain of losing him.

Dean threw the heavy book down on his desk and rose abruptly to his feet. He hadn't seen Whitney in four days; she was even refusing to take his calls. Every time he telephoned Sweet House, Anne Grant would tell him, in her stiffly polite voice, that her daughter was indisposed and couldn't possibly come to the phone.

"Stubborn idiot," he muttered.

He had never been so exasperated with her. And although he hated to admit it, he had never been so worried, either. Dean had been so sure she wouldn't stay angry with him. But now, since he couldn't talk to her, he didn't know if she was simply sulking or genuinely hurt.

Rubbing the back of his neck, he walked to the window that looked out over the backyard, his gaze lingering on the flowers she had planted there.

He missed her, he admitted reluctantly. Whitney had been a part of his life for so long. A big part of his life. When he grew angry with the legal system— something that happened often—or when he became too deeply involved in a case, Whitney was always there to take his mind off his problems. Somehow, at some point in the past, he had come to depend on her.

As he leaned his forehead against the glass, he tried to figure out why he felt so uneasy. It wasn't as though he was in the habit of seeing Whitney every day. They had been separated plenty of times—when she was in college, and when the Harcourts, en masse, went traveling. Several times a year they would take off for parts unknown to mingle with other wealthy, traveling folk.

Why, then, did Dean feel that this separation was different? Why did he feel as though there was an emotional as well as physical distance between them?

When the doorbell rang Dean turned away from the window and frowned. It couldn't be Whitney. She never bothered with ringing the bell. Since the house had become his, she always just walked in.

On the other hand, maybe this was her way of showing that she remembered his angry demands for privacy.

It wasn't Whitney.

Anne Grant was the last person Dean would expect to find on his doorstep—she had always made a point of ignoring him if they happened to pass by each other on the street, as though she didn't want to acknowledge the fact that Dean even existed—but here she was, standing on his front porch.

"Mrs. Grant," he said, carefully keeping his expression neutral. "What can I do for you?"

She didn't meet his eyes. She looked around his porch—anywhere but at him—as she fidgeted with the clutch purse she held in gloved hands. "I need to talk to you," she said, her voice characteristically faint.

Opening the door wider, he waved her inside. "Sure. Come in."

After he had shown the woman to an armchair in the living room, he sat down and studied her, waiting for her to tell him what this was all about. Her uneasiness was evident in her posture. Anne Grant had always been stiff around him, but today she was positively rigid.

"You— Your home is charming," she said finally. "You've done a beautiful job of restoration."

"Thank you." He wanted to tell her to either fish or cut bait, but he knew that would make her even more uncomfortable. "How's Whitney? Is she still 'indisposed'?"

Anne immediately dropped her gaze to her hands. "My daughter is the reason I'm here today," she said with obvious reluctance.

Dean was instantly alert. A new element had crept into the woman's vague voice, an element that brought apprehension into the room with them.

"What about Whitney?" Tension gripped the muscles in his neck and shoulders, but he kept his voice calm. "Where is she? Whitney's all right, isn't she? She's not really sick or—"

"She's gone."

For a moment Dean wasn't sure he had heard the soft words correctly. "What the hell are you talking about?" Politeness discarded, his voice was now harsh and abrupt. "What do you mean, she's gone?"

"She left sometime in the middle of the night on Sunday. I knew she was upset, but I didn't expect this. She simply packed her bags and walked out." When her lips trembled slightly, she pursed them and continued. "She didn't even leave a note for me."

Dean stood up, turning away from her as he raked his fingers through his hair. Packed her bags? Walked out? Whitney was gone? Whitney was *gone*.

"Did she speak to you about our...disagreement?" Anne Grant asked.

He turned back to the woman, his thoughts chaotic. Whitney's mother still wouldn't meet his eyes, but when he didn't answer, she added, "I knew she was on her way to see you when I saw her go through the hedge." Her lips tightened again. "Since she was a little girl, she has always come to you when something upsets her."

How she hated admitting that, he thought, then glanced away from her rigid features.

"She told me nothing."

The words were low and tight with anger, but this time the anger was directed toward himself. Whitney hadn't had the chance to tell him anything. Damn it, he should have known something was wrong with her that day. *He should have known something had hurt her.*

Dean had spent the past four days pushing the picture of how she looked in his bedroom out of his mind, but now he forcibly called it up.

There had been a wild look in her blue eyes that day, as though she were frightened and confused. It was the same way she had looked on the day he'd found her sitting on the curb so many years ago, only worse. What had happened to her? What had the Harcourts done to her? And why in hell hadn't he at least given her a chance to talk?

"She told me nothing," he repeated wearily.

Mrs. Grant shifted her position slightly. "My daughter found—" She broke off and gave her head a little shake. "Whitney has decided that her father is still alive. As a result—"

"What are you talking about?" he interrupted. "You're not making sense. Your husband drowned in a boating accident almost twenty years ago. Whitney knew that. Why should she suddenly take a notion that he's alive?"

Anne Grant didn't answer. She simply held herself even more stiffly as she stared at a painting hanging on the opposite wall. Then, when the silence had almost become a physical thing between them, Whitney's mother shifted her gaze to her white-gloved hands and said, "Mr. Russell, I came to you because I need your help."

He studied her for a long time, then shook his head in amazement. "You're a real piece of work. Her father *is* alive, isn't he? And Whitney found out that you've been keeping the truth from her for all these years. Judas Priest, lady, what kind of mother are you?"

Her head bobbed just a little, as though she had taken a blow. "What I did, I did for the best."

"Whose best?" he asked in contempt. "Yours? Certainly not your daughter's." He swung away from her, rage tightening his throat. "You're just like all the other Harcourts. You ignore what you don't want to see. An inconvenient husband?" He gave a short laugh. "Hell, that's easy. Just kill him off. Pretend he doesn't exist...the same way you've always pretended I don't exist."

Her peach complexion turned ruddy as she finally met his eyes. Her anger was out in the open now, and the cast-iron center was exposed. "What did you expect?" she said, her voice hoarse with emotion. "Was I supposed to accept the fact that my daughter—a sweet uncomplicated child—was running with a wild boy from Trash Town? Did you think I would be pleased about that?"

"That was years ago, Mrs. Grant," he said with quiet but equal intensity. "I'm not a boy anymore, and Trash Town no longer exists."

"But you are still *you*. Oh, I knew what she was doing. I've always known. You were nothing more than a form of rebellion for my daughter. If I had been smart, if I had known it would *last,* I would have told her I thought you were absolutely wonderful and that I objected to one of the boys she knew who came from a good family. Because if I had done that, Mr. Russell, you can be sure Whitney would have attached herself to him instead."

Dean didn't want to listen. He tried to tell himself that the woman was speaking out of spite, out of anger, but it was no use. The words twisted through his insides and settled in a hard knot in his stomach.

He had no comeback for her. He didn't want to admit that the same thought had occurred to him years ago.

They continued to stare at each other, matching anger with anger, until Dean had finally had enough. This asinine squabbling was getting them nowhere. It certainly wasn't helping Whitney.

Sweet heaven, she must have been crushed by her mother's betrayal. And his own, he thought, feeling the knot twist tighter. She must have felt as though the world had blown apart around her.

"You said you needed my help," he said, smiling grimly at the irony of her request. Anne Grant despised him, yet she had come to him for help. "I assume you want me to find her. Well, I accept the job. But before I even start looking, I need to know why she left. Was it to get away from you and the Harcourts, or was it to find her father?"

Dean felt a grudging respect for the woman's strength when he saw that she didn't even flinch at the obvious insult.

"She doesn't know where to look," she said after a moment. "I burned all the... Whitney doesn't know where to look," she repeated, her voice and expression growing vague again.

Dean laughed, but there was no amusement in the sound. "Burned all the evidence, did you? I wouldn't count on that stopping Whitney. You apparently don't know your daughter very well, Mrs. Grant. She's not only sharp-witted, she's one of the most outrageously stubborn people I've ever come across." He shook his head. "No, Whit won't give up easily. She especially doesn't give up on people."

Unless she thinks they're giving up on her, he thought as his own words called up that terrible scene in his bedroom.

Setting his jaw, Dean shook the vision away. He couldn't think of that now.

"She told me that you never talked about your husband," he continued slowly, "so out of respect for you, she didn't mention him at home. But she mentioned him here, Mrs. Grant. I bet I could describe him to you, down to the last detail. And I could tell you, also in detail, how much Whitney loved him. How much she still loves him."

He shook his head. "No, if there was one chance in a million that she could have her father back, she'd take it, no matter what she had to do."

He paused, waiting for Whitney's mother to meet his eyes. When she did, he said, "Where would she look, Mrs. Grant?"

She made a soft noise of protest and shook her head in a helpless movement.

"Where would she look?" he repeated, his voice growing harder. "Come on, lady, if your husband hadn't been killed nineteen years ago in a boating accident, where do you think he would be living right now?"

She dropped her gaze to her hands. At some point she had taken off her gloves, but instead of folding them neatly, she was twisting them between her fingers with agitated little movements.

"Dallas," she whispered at last. "Whitney might be in Dallas."

"Dallas," he repeated, finding it both sad and absurd that she still hadn't admitted her husband was alive.

"Please find her, Mr. Russell." Anne Grant rose gracefully to her feet. "Find her and bring her home."

"I'll find her," he said as he walked her to the door. "But I can't force her to come back. Whitney is an adult now. She has to make her own choices."

As soon as he closed the door behind Anne Grant, Dean picked up the telephone and punched in the number of someone he knew in the district attorney's office. He would ask his friend to check to see if Whitney was using her credit cards. That would tell Dean if she was, in fact, in Dallas.

Next he called Boedecker and Kraus and discovered that Whitney had canceled her interview, a fact that bothered him even more than the way she had left. Packing up and leaving in the middle of the night sounded like a whim. But taking the time to call and cancel a job interview sounded more planned, more permanent somehow.

Dean's last call was to his office. "Listen, Sam," he said when his partner came on the line, "I need you to take over for me next week."

Fifteen minutes later he replaced the receiver and leaned against the wall. He'd told Anne Grant that her daughter was an adult. Dean truly believed that, and he would fight for her right to make her own decisions. But he also knew how vulnerable Whitney was. She had never been totally on her own before, and she wasn't prepared for the real world. She was too innocent, too trusting for her own good, and Dean was scared out of his mind for her.

Sweet heaven, Whitney, he thought, what have you gotten yourself into this time?

Chapter Six

Rick's Pub wasn't exactly in the wealthy section of Dallas. In fact, it wasn't exactly in the middle-class section, either. In Rick's part of town, it was strictly low rent.

The area around the small pub contained a few well-kept housing developments, but most of the land was taken up by aging apartment complexes and row after row of tiny frame houses.

There were no shopping malls or chichi boutiques here. The businesses around Rale Street were like the houses and the people. Basic. Utilitarian. An area resident could buy car parts or industrial cleaning supplies without leaving the vicinity. He could even rent a backhoe if he wanted. But anyone planning a gala or redecorating a home would have to look in another part of town.

The bar sat on an imaginary line that separated the residential district to the north from the industrial row that lay to the south. Like the houses and the people, Rick's Pub was pretty basic. There were no flashing lights, no revolving glitter balls, just a mirrored bar, a jukebox and lots of bare wooden tables.

It came equipped with a bouncer—a giant that everyone called Tink—but the man never seemed to leave his barstool. If anyone in the bar became too rowdy, the other patrons either calmed the troublemaker down or ejected him themselves. Rick's was their special place, and they allowed nothing to disrupt their time there.

The men and women who gathered each evening at the bar worked on loading docks and assembly lines. They weren't a pretentious group. These people were blue-collar and proud of it.

Everyone knew everyone at Rick's. Occasionally an outsider might wander in, but the majority of the customers were people who had been coming to the bar for years. They lived and worked and played in this area. They raised their families here. It was the warmth, the camaraderie of the patrons, that gave Rick's Pub its own special charm.

However, after spending three days sitting on a barstool, the charm of the place was beginning to wear a little thin for Whitney. Being an outsider didn't bother her so much, and she didn't mind the curious stares and whispered debates about whether or not she was the new girl who handled invoices at the paper factory. She even thought it was sort of funny when the bouncer had hinted, in a perfectly kind voice, that prostitutes weren't allowed in Rick's. But in the past three days she had drunk enough club soda to float a battleship, and she still hadn't seen anyone who vaguely resembled her father.

Whitney always arrived at the bar early in the afternoon, and after ordering a drink, she would surreptitiously examine the face of each male who entered the bar. She had spotted several men who were big enough or tall enough—men with black hair and blue eyes—to be her father, but unfortunately all of the features never came together on any one man.

She realized he might not have kept the mustache she remembered, and since he would be in his mid-fifties now, he probably had some gray in his hair—her imagination placed just a touch of silver at his temples—but even if there were physical changes she hadn't anticipated, Whitney was positive she would recognize his voice. Lloyd Grant's voice had been unmistakable. He was a powerful man with a powerful speaking voice and a big, booming laugh.

Sighing wistfully, she swung around on the stool and gazed into the mirror behind the bar. It was four o'clock, which meant the men who worked at the toy factory would be coming in soon. There were five of them, regulars who came in every day. Whitney liked them. Not that she had formally met any one of them, but she had listened to the outrageous stories they told and had heard them rock with laughter. They laughed a lot.

At the moment there were only four other people in the bar. Two women in their early thirties—who had spent the past hour gossiping about a neighbor going through a messy divorce—and two men. Whitney had never seen the men before and didn't know if they were regulars who had been away for a while, or if they were entirely new to the bar.

Business at Rick's was always a little slow until the shifts started changing at the factories. After that, people would arrive in groups both small and large.

As the women paid for their drinks and stood up to leave, Whitney noticed that the two men were watching her, and one of them had an unmistakable question in his eyes as he slowly examined her.

Glancing away from them, she stifled a laugh. It had suddenly occurred to her that they might have mistaken her for a "working girl," the way Tink had.

That particular idea still struck Whitney as ridiculous. She was wearing faded jeans and an old S.M.U. sweatshirt; her hair was in a loose French braid, and she wore no makeup other than lipstick. She'd always thought prostitutes would have a little more flash to them.

Shifting her eyes again to the mirror, she saw the men from the toy factory enter the bar. The same five came every day. Two of them were twins, not identical, but alike enough to be recognizable as such. The third was fortyish, and had bright red hair and freckles that covered every visible inch of flesh. The fourth, much older than the others, was thin and stoop-shouldered and had a shock of white hair, only slightly less wild than Albert Einstein's. The fifth appeared to be about the age her father would be now, but he was short, plump and almost completely bald.

Whitney watched as each man entered, then suddenly she sat up straighter. There was someone new with them today. A big man. A man who had hair as dark as Whitney's.

Swallowing with difficulty, she studied the new man. His age was hard to judge. While he appeared to be in his forties, he could have been one of those people who never showed their true age.

It was possible, she thought. This man was a definite possibility. If only she could see his eyes or hear him speak, then she would know for sure. Maybe if she dropped something, he would turn and—

"Dumpling, you've got the sweetest set of knockers I've seen lately."

Startled, Whitney glanced around and found one of the men from the corner table at her elbow.

"I beg your pardon?" she said, her chin raising automatically.

"I said you've got a great set of knockers," he repeated distinctly, a grin spreading across his face.

Whitney let her gaze drift over him with slow deliberation. "I hope you haven't spent a lot of time practicing that line," she said as she turned her back on him, "because I have to tell you, it still needs work."

He laughed and leaned closer. "Hot for me already, aren't you? My name's Will. Why don't we blow this joint and go back to my place?"

"I don't think so," she said, moving away from him to slide off the opposite side of the stool.

She didn't get far. Her way was blocked by Will's friend, who stood on her side, watching her with detached, almost lazy, interest.

Whitney wasn't frightened; she had come to trust the people in the bar and knew they wouldn't let these men cause any trouble. But she was becoming annoyed that they were blocking her view of the men from the toy factory.

Raising her head, she met Will's eyes. "Let me clue you in," she said, heaving a sigh of exasperation. "And I want you to listen carefully because I *never* repeat myself. I wouldn't leave this bar with you if the place were on fire and you had the key to the only exit. Got it?"

Apparently he didn't get it at all because, with the same stupid grin on his face, he began to run his hand up her back. Gritting her teeth, Whitney looked down the bar toward the bouncer's stool, then blinked in startled reaction.

For the first time since she had been coming to Rick's Pub, the big man's barstool was unoccupied. Tink had left his post.

Uneasiness finally set in, and Whitney swiveled her head toward the table where the group from the toy factory always sat, but except for the old man with the Albert Einstein hair, the table was empty. The others all stood around the dart board at the back of the room.

"Would you stop that?" she ground out as Will began to run his hand over her back again. When he simply laughed once more, Whitney drew in a deep breath, preparing to scream.

"That's enough. You guys have had your fun. Now it's time for you to leave."

Whitney almost fell off the barstool. She knew that voice. She had heard it when she was a child. She had heard it in her dreams.

Instantly she forgot about the irritating men on either side of her and turned her head slowly to follow the voice. When she saw the white-haired man standing close to the bar, her gaze went quickly beyond him as she searched for her father. But there was no one else there.

"You gonna make us, old man?"

Will's belligerent question had Whitney swinging her gaze back to the white-haired man.

"*Tink!*" the old man's voice boomed out.

Whitney's vision blurred and she felt weak. His voice was strong and powerful. It was unmistakable.

"Is there a problem here?"

She heard the bouncer's voice; she saw him standing just a foot away, but somehow Whitney had become separated from the scene, separated from reality. Ignoring all else, she could only stare. This was Lloyd Grant? This was her father?

"No problems, Tink," the old man said. "These gentlemen were just leaving."

"So soon? Here, I'll show y'all to the door." Tink grabbed each man by the upper arm and began to walk them both toward the pub's entrance. "I don't want you boys to be strangers now." They were wincing from the big man's tight grip. "You won't find a friendlier place than Rick's," the bouncer added as he tossed them out the door.

When the door swung shut behind them, Tink turned to make his way back to his regular barstool. As he passed Whitney and the older gent, he nodded. "Ma'am . . . Lloyd," he said before easing his massive frame back onto the stool.

When her father turned away from her, when he began to move away, Whitney finally found herself back in reality.

"Wait," she called out, the word breathless and abrupt.

She had to get her brain back in gear. She had to form words, a whole sentence, before he got away from her.

He glanced over his shoulder at her and she said, "I—I didn't thank you for coming to my rescue."

He shrugged away her gratitude. "I didn't do anything. I just stalled them until Tink got back from the john," he replied, turning away again.

His voice was different now, softer. The strength in it had disappeared. But his voice didn't matter. Tink had called him Lloyd, and that was all the confirmation Whitney needed.

Clenching her hands into fists to keep them from shaking, she drew in a deep breath and hopped off the barstool to follow him. "Mr.— I'm sorry, I didn't catch your name."

He sat down at the empty table. "Lloyd," he said in a tone that clearly stated, whether she liked it or not, that this conversation was finished.

He didn't know that Whitney had always taken great pride in being contrary. "Mr. Lloyd?"

"Just Lloyd."

"Well, Just Lloyd, you saved my bacon, whether you want to admit it or not. And that means I owe you a drink." She hailed a waitress. "What do you drink? Is that beer? Roxie," she said to the blond waitress, "bring Just Lloyd another beer and I'll have—"

"Club soda?" Roxie offered.

Whitney laughed. "No, I'm feeling adventurous. Bring me a glass of white wine."

"Sure you can handle it?" the waitress said dryly as she turned away.

Whitney returned her gaze to Lloyd and found him watching her. There was curiosity in his blue eyes, but he asked no questions.

She smiled. "You're wondering what you got yourself into, aren't you?" she asked cheerfully. "Right now you're thinking 'Why didn't I mind my own business?' Well, for the past three days I've watched everyone in this bar having fun while you've been sitting here minding your own business. But in my opinion, if you spend your whole life not getting involved, you might look up one day and realize that you've opted out, that you're not a part of life anymore, and that your own business is a lonely place."

He stared at her for a moment. "Do you always talk this much?"

"Yes," she admitted readily. "It drives everyone I know crazy. But I do respond to 'shut up.' Sometimes."

"Shut up, what? You didn't give me your name."

She blinked twice. She couldn't tell him her real name. Not now. He finally seemed to be loosening up a little, and if she told him who she was he could very well start backing away from her again.

Roxie chose that moment to bring the drinks, which gave Whitney time to frantically search for a new name. Something cute and perky? Something exotic?

Bright and beautiful and full of life is my Maid Mary.

"Mary," she said, then, glancing at his hair, added, "Mary White."

"So what are you doing in this part of town, Mary? What are you running away from?"

She choked on her wine. "I don't know what you're talking about," she said when she stopped coughing.

His gaze drifted over her face. "Your clothes are old, but you won't find many people in Rick's who went to S.M.U. And it wouldn't matter if you were wearing a feed sack. You look expensive. The way you carry yourself. The way you talk. Even your haircut looks expensive." His lips twisted in what was almost a smile. "If you're ticked off at your parents, you could have found a softer place to run away to."

Her chin went up. "I'm over twenty-one," she said, then, hearing the sulky note in her voice, she smiled.

"Circumstances forced me to change my life-style. Haven't you ever heard of anyone down on their luck? And believe it or not, I can take care of myself."

"Yeah, I saw."

His skepticism irritated her. "Look, I've been in here for three days and—"

"Why?"

She frowned. "I beg your pardon?"

"Why have you been in here for three days? Sitting at the bar, watching everyone that comes in, eaves-dropping on our conversations. Why?"

She moistened her lips in a nervous gesture. "I don't know, I guess I was just looking for companionship. Sitting here, listening to the regulars having a good time, that was nice." She shook her head. "Anyway, after three days I knew what kind of people came here. I knew all I had to do was yell and your friends at the dart board would have helped me."

He listened but he made no comment, and as silence fell between them, she could feel her father slipping away from her again, retreating to a place she couldn't reach.

Panicking, she leaned toward him. "As a matter of fact, I guess you *could* say I'm running away from someone."

As she'd hoped, the confession caught his attention. He raised his gaze from his glass and looked at her. "I knew it," he said quietly.

"But not my parents. A man." *The* man, she corrected silently, and the thought of Dean brought a tight pain to her chest.

"I've loved him all my life," she continued, her voice soft and husky. "His name is Dean. Don't you think that's a good name. A perfect name." She took a sip of wine. "The bad part is, he doesn't love me back. I thought he cared— No, he did care. But caring's not enough, is it? After I thought about it, I realized he's been trying to tell me for a long time that he would never love me, at least not the way I need him to. I just wouldn't listen. I didn't *want* to listen. I didn't want to hear the truth. I kept telling myself that someday—"

She broke off and shook her head. "It's funny how Someday can be the most wonderful concept, and yet also be a crippling thing. If you get too busy focusing on someday, you neglect the here and now." Her lips twisted in a self-mocking smile. "Which is, of course, what I did. So when everything fell apart, I was left with nothing. I had bet the whole paycheck on Dean."

She leaned back in her seat, her head tilted back slightly as the memory of that day came back to her. "There was a . . . a confrontation, and he—"

She sat up straighter and met Lloyd's eyes. "Dean's a kind man. Don't ever think he's not. It's just that suddenly he'd had enough. Of me, I guess. He'd had enough of the way I hung onto him." She shrugged. "I took him by surprise, and he let his real feelings show. All this time, he's seen me as a burden."

She grimaced. "The truth isn't always fun, but it's certainly enlightening. I just couldn't take the thought of seeing him all the time, knowing how he felt about me."

She paused to draw in a deep, shaky breath. "So I guess you could say I'm running away from myself. From what I was on my way to becoming." She put her elbows on the table and propped her chin in her palms. "So what do you think? Am I a mess or what?"

Her companion threw back his head and laughed, which delighted her. It was the laugh that she had heard in her memories. Maybe not quite as strong as it had once been, but there was still a soaring quality to it.

"You're something, that's for sure," he said, still chuckling. "Are you sure you didn't simply talk him into a stupor?"

She grinned. "I probably did that, too."

He raised his arm and looked at her across the beer mug as he took a swallow. "Do you really want my opinion?" he asked as he lowered the mug.

"I do," she said earnestly. "I really do."

"I think you've saved yourself a lot of heartache," he said flatly. "I'm alone and most of the time I think it's the best way. No responsibilities, no one to disappoint. Because that's where the real pain comes from, Mary. Not from what's been done to you, but from what you've done to others. That's the part that will rip you apart."

What did you do? she wanted to ask. But she knew she couldn't. What she saw in his eyes wasn't pain from the past. It was from the present.

Did he feel, even after all these years, guilty for having walked out on his family? The thought made her throat constrict with suppressed emotion. She had suffered because of his desertion, but her grief was nothing compared to what this man had gone through.

Like Prometheus, this man's pain was endless. Day after day, it rose up fresh and new, to torment him.

He rose abruptly to his feet. "I'd better be going," he said, his voice gruff.

Whitney knew Lloyd never left Rick's until ten, but she made no move to stop him. She had reminded him of something that hurt, something he wanted to deal with in private. And in truth, she could use some time of her own to think.

"Thanks for the drink." Lloyd turned to leave, then he paused. "You looking for a job?"

The question took her by surprise. She stared at him for a moment, then nodded slowly. "Now that you mention it, I believe I am."

"There's an opening at the factory. I can put in a good word for you if you want."

"Thank you, Just Lloyd. I would appreciate that." She grinned. "I can use all the good words I can get."

With a soft chuckle, he walked away.

Whitney watched as the door swung shut behind him, then closed her eyes. She had almost told him. Right there at the end, when she realized how much he was hurting, she had almost told him that she was his daughter.

The words had been on the tip of her tongue when she realized that she didn't know a thing about this man. The pain she saw in him might not have anything to do with the family he had left behind. She had no way of knowing if he even remembered he had a daughter. After all, people left their families behind all the time, cheerfully and without regret.

So in the end, it was fear that kept her mouth shut. She was afraid that if she told him who she was, he would walk away and never look back.

She would wait until she knew him better. She would let him get to know her as an individual, let him see that she was no threat to him or the new life he had made for himself.

Whitney was pushing back the chair to stand up when it finally hit her.

She had found her father.

Beginning a new life was hard work, and the next few days were busy ones for Whitney. She was more or less helpless when it came to looking for an apartment, choosing furniture and buying groceries, and she made sure Lloyd knew it. Every time he tried to back away from her—and he tried quite often at first—Whitney, without a twinge of conscience, begged for his help.

"In China," she told him, "when you save a person's life, you have to assume responsibility for that person. It's a law, Lloyd. Check it out."

"All I did was yell for Tink to throw out some troublemakers," he said, laughing at her outrageous exaggerating. "I didn't save your life."

"You did," she argued. "You saved my life. Because if that fool had touched me one more time, I would have cold-cocked him with a seltzer bottle. And if he had gotten a concussion and died, I'd have been arrested for using unreasonable force and any jury in the world would have found me guilty, because it's obvious that I did it. What's more, I don't see how I could possibly show any remorse, and you know how judges feel about penitence.'' Her voice dropped ominously. ''They give lethal injections in Texas, Lloyd.''

''Okay...okay, I give up. I'll help you pick out your stupid pots and pans.''

Lloyd not only helped her pick out pots and pans, he took her to the places that sold good used furniture, then he rounded up enough volunteers with pickup trucks to move the furniture into the small apartment she had rented in his building.

Occasionally Whitney worried about getting cash from her credit cards, knowing the bills were going to her uncle, but she was keeping an account of every dollar she spent. She would be able to support herself soon, then she would begin paying her uncle back. It was suddenly important that she make her own way in the world. She wanted her father to be proud of her. She wanted to be proud of herself.

The one area in which she couldn't ask for Lloyd's help was her new job. At the factory, Whitney was on her own.

The first obstacle was a simple little detail that threatened to ruin the whole scheme—Whitney's name and social security number.

She had watched the people at Rick's long enough to know the toy factory was like a small town. There were no secrets. If Whitney gave her true name, it would be all over the factory within hours. But if she used her new name and a fictitious social security number, she was pretty sure the federal government wouldn't like it.

The dilemma had kept her pacing outside the personnel office for hours on the day she was supposed to apply for a job. Just as Whitney had decided she would have to forget the whole thing, the woman who ran the office came back from lunch.

With her blue hair and faded housedress, Mrs. Dennison looked like everyone's grandmother. But looks were deceiving. Lloyd had told Whitney about Mrs. Dennison. She was the owner's mother, and nothing happened in the factory without her permission. But what gave Whitney hope wasn't the sweet grandmotherly face or the power the woman wielded. What made Whitney follow Mrs. Dennison into the personnel office was the paperback book the older woman carried under her arm. *Midland Mafia Murders*. Mrs. Dennison was a true crime fan.

An hour later Whitney not only had a new job, but a promise from her new friend that no one would ever know her real name.

Whitney hadn't actually lied to Mrs. Dennison. She'd simply told her about her wish to start a new life, throwing in a few hints that if certain people knew where Whitney was hiding, "things" might happen. Things that simply couldn't be talked about. So it would be better, safer for everyone concerned, if no one at the factory knew Whitney's real name.

Mrs. Dennison had eaten up every word.

The second obstacle wasn't so easily resolved. The fact that Lloyd Grant, a much admired supervisor, had recommended Whitney for the job helped her make friends quickly, but not even a recommendation from the president would have helped her on the assembly line.

It was Whitney's job to attach little rubber tires to little toy trucks, and when Lloyd had described the task, it had sounded like a snap. After all, how difficult could it be?

She learned the answer to that question on her first day at the toy factory. Attaching little rubber tires to little toy trucks could be pure, unadulterated hell. Everyone had neglected to tell her the job had to be done at top speed.

The first day felt a little like she had been dropped into an old *I Love Lucy* episode. The trucks seemed to come at her faster and faster. She would barely have time to get one tire on—forget the other three—before another truck descended on her.

That night Whitney had nightmares about all those little red and blue and yellow trucks chasing her, demanding not only tires, but a lube job, as well.

By her third day at the factory, Whitney had begun to adjust. She still wasn't as fast as she should be, but she was beginning to believe that someday, if she worked hard at it, she might eventually be adequate.

She tried to talk Lloyd into car-pooling. It made no sense to take both cars, she told him. They would have each other's company on the ride to and from work, and save gas, as well. It was practically their civic duty.

But in this one matter, Lloyd held out. Sharing a car somehow represented a closeness he wasn't ready to acknowledge.

It didn't take Whitney long to understand why everyone went to Rick's after work. The pressure at the factory was intense. They needed to relax and let off steam before going home to normal life.

On Friday night, after her first week at the factory, everyone was at Rick's for the weekly dart tournament. Whitney had played every once in a while with Lloyd and a few of her new friends, and it was at their urging that she decided to enter the tournament.

She took her first two opponents easily, and her last match was with Frankie Halloran, self-acknowledged Lothario. Frankie—tanned and muscular, with dark, curly hair—thought a lot of himself, but he was too likable for people to take any real offense at his conceit.

"It's my turn, little Miss Dart Shark. I think I can take you, and I'm willing to back that up with a little side bet."

Frankie's challenge brought on a chorus of derisive hoots.

"Okay, here's the deal," he continued. "If I win, you go with me to the tractor pull tomorrow night...and parking afterward," he added with an overdone leer.

"And if I win?" she asked.

"Make him polish that ratty old Buick of yours," someone called out.

"No, make him scrub your kitchen floor," one of the women suggested. "And take pictures. You could make a fortune selling pictures of Frankie on his knees."

When everyone laughed, Frankie held up a hand to quiet them. "If you win," he said, "I'll buy a round of drinks for everybody in the place."

"Go for it, Mary."

"Make him pay."

"Didn't Rick get in a shipment of imported beer yesterday?"

"You can take him," Lloyd said as he stepped closer and raised his voice to be heard over the enthusiastic crowd. "Just keep your distance. He has a habit of brushing against you just when you're ready to throw."

Although everyone wanted a free drink, when the game started, the group divided into two groups. The young, single men and a few of the single women—the ones who were hoping to date Frankie—were rooting for Whitney's opponent. The others were cheering for her.

Whitney knew immediately that Frankie was good, better than any of the others she had played against, but she kept her cool.

"Come on, Mary, you can do it. Show him your stuff. Make him eat your dust."

Whitney picked up another dart and turned to wave at the bouncer, who was cheering her on from his barstool. She'd learned that Tink was short for Tinkerbell, and considered the fact that he didn't mind the nickname a sign of the big man's self-confidence.

"Stop distracting her," Lloyd called to Tink before turning back to Whitney. He stood at the forefront of the crowd gathered around the dart board. "Take your time, Mary. This shot has to be good."

In a show of total self-assurance, she dusted a bit of lint from her sleeve, then casually tossed the dart in the air and watched it hit dead center.

Whitney was immediately surrounded by the group. They were all pounding her on the back, shouting their approval, taunting her opponent.

When Whitney saw Frankie taking the teasing with a good-natured grin, she stood on her tiptoes and kissed him on the cheek. "Your consolation prize," she said.

Laughing, he grabbed her around the waist and leaned her over backward. The kiss was long and noisy, and even though it was more playful than sexual, it brought cheers and enthusiastic encouragement from the rest of the crowd.

When Frankie finally turned her loose, Whitney made a big play of wiping her face before turning to signal Roxie for a drink. Her hand was in the air and her mouth was open to speak when her eyes widened in shock.

Dean was standing not three feet away from her. And judging by the look on his face, there was going to be hell to pay.

Chapter Seven

Whitney's mind went completely blank, becoming nothing more than an empty space between her ears. Then, with dizzying abruptness, her brain began working overtime. Dean was here. In Dallas. At Rick's.

His expensive suit looked out of place in the pub, and Whitney's new friends were beginning to stare. They were beginning to speculate.

"Internal Revenue?" someone proposed.

"No, he's too good-looking."

Someone else suggested a pimp, but that was quickly knocked down by the fact that he wore no gold jewelry. Although several were positive he was simply lost, the determined look in his dark eyes seemed to quash that theory. It eventually boiled down to a tie between a Mafia hit man and a real estate developer who wanted to buy the place, tear it down and build something more profitable.

At any other time Whitney would have seen the humor in the situation and thrown in her own outrageous theories, but at the moment she was too busy panicking.

How had he found her? And what was more important, *why* had he found her? If Dean approached her, using her real name, everything she had worked so hard to accomplish would be lost. It couldn't happen. Too much was at stake.

Forcing herself to meet Dean's eyes, she gave her head a little shake. Let him understand, she begged silently. Please let him understand.

She shouldn't have doubted him. After only the slightest pause, he moved to sit at the bar and ordered a drink, his expression now suitably blank.

"Dean?"

Whitney swung around, her heart pounding. Lloyd was standing beside her, studying her face carefully.

"What did you say?" she asked, her voice faint with panic.

"I asked if that was your Dean."

If there had been one chance in a million of getting away with it, Whitney would have denied everything. But already Lloyd was coming to know her. He would have spotted the lie in an instant.

"Not mine." Her lips curved in a wry smile. "He never was mine. But it's Dean all right." She paused to draw in a slow breath. "It's definitely Dean."

Lloyd glanced toward the bar. "He didn't look pleased."

"No," she agreed weakly, "he didn't, did he?"

Lloyd led her back to their table, gently pushing her into a chair. "If he sees you as a burden, why did he bother to track you down?"

She caught her lower lip between her teeth, then gave her head a little shake. "I guess because he thinks I'm *his* burden. I told you he was kind. He's been taking care of me—getting me out of trouble, being my foundation—since I was six years old." She paused, gathering her thoughts. "He never wanted me to just disappear. But he wanted me to have a life of my own, which I have now. Of course, he couldn't know that. And that's why he's here...maybe," she finished without conviction.

"Are you going to talk to him?"

She shook her head vigorously. "Not now. It's not that I'm a coward, I just prefer to be humiliated in private."

Lloyd frowned, glancing at Dean again. "Will he try to humiliate you?"

"No," she admitted, "but he won't have to. I usually manage to do just fine on my own." With difficulty she pulled her gaze away from Dean. "Let's talk about something else. If I ignore him, maybe he'll go away."

Her father chuckled. "Somehow I don't think he's the type to conveniently vanish."

Lloyd was wrong. A few minutes later Dean paid for his drink and slid off the barstool. On his way out, although he passed within a foot of the table where she sat, he didn't acknowledge her with so much as a glance.

When the door closed behind him, when she no longer felt his presence in the room, Whitney should have been able to relax and join in the conversation that flowed around her, but it wasn't that easy. One glimpse of him and she was a mess, electrified and confused, exhilarated and apprehensive.

After she left San Antonio, Whitney told herself she would be able to put her love for him in the past where it belonged, and go on from there. She told herself that loving Dean would be a part of the Whitney Daryn Grant she'd moved away from. Like the white Jaguar, her love for Dean would always be there, but it would be safely in storage. A memory. A piece of the past, one of many, that helped set her on the way to becoming the new Whitney Daryn Grant.

Then she realized the truth. She was a fool. A thousand times a fool. Her love for Dean wasn't in storage, and it wasn't a bit of nostalgia. It was right here in her heart, as strong and deep and solid as ever. She had simply been hiding from it.

As of tonight, there was no place left to hide.

"I guess it's time for me to get home," Lloyd said, breaking into her thoughts.

Dismayed, she glanced at her watch. How could it be ten already? She wasn't ready for the evening to be over. She wasn't ready to leave this place with its comforting shield of noise and laughter.

Rising reluctantly to her feet, she walked with Lloyd to the entrance, waving good-night to friends who called out to them. Outside the bar Lloyd squeezed her hand, told her good-night and disappeared into the shadows of the parking lot.

Whitney stood for a moment and glanced around. Drawing in a deep, steadying breath, she straightened her shoulders and walked toward her car.

She was in the process of unlocking the Buick when someone grabbed her from behind. A hand came over her mouth, cutting off her squeaking gasp, and she was lifted off her feet. With his free hand, her assailant opened the car door, shoved her inside, and slid in beside her, forcibly moving her over to make room for him. Seconds later she was in her attacker's arms, being ruthlessly kissed. Then, before she had time to either respond or repel, she was being pushed away.

"Do you see what could happen to you?" Dean rasped out, his breathing harsh as he gave her one hard shake.

Oh, yes, she thought, *he's definitely ticked off.*

The light from the parking lot barely made it into the car, but Whitney didn't have to see him to know he was shaking with fury.

"Do you see how easy it would be for someone to hurt you?" he went on. "Damn it, Whitney, you didn't even struggle. You didn't even try to scream. You simply— What? What did you say?''

"I said I knew it was you." She wiped her mouth with the back of her hand, anger building in her, as well. "I knew you would be out here. And I knew you were mad."

"Mad? *Mad?* That doesn't even come close to describing how I feel. What in holy hell do you think you're doing? Do you know how scared your mother is? And your uncle—" He broke off and gave a short laugh as he raked a hand through his hair. "Your distinguished uncle has very quietly, very discreetly, gone right around the bend. He's been calling out the FBI, the CIA, Pinkerton's and the *sainted Mounted Police!* Where is the Jaguar? Why in hell are you driving a car that's older than you are? Damn it, Whitney, do you have any idea what you've done? I've been chasing after you for over a week. My practice is going down the tubes and I can't do a damn thing about it because I'm too busy wandering around skid row hunting for you."

"Who asked you to?" she demanded through clenched teeth. "Do you see me sending up smoke signals? I was doing just fine. At least I was until you strolled in looking like a Wall Street version of James Bond. I can take care of myself, thank you very much. And like I said, who asked you?"

Dean stared at her face in the dim light. She had that look he remembered so well. Stubborn, rebellious. God, it was good to see her. He hadn't dreamed it would take so long to catch up with her, and each day that had passed without finding her had intensified his fear. He had told himself that when he found her he would kill her. But first he would hold her so tight that she wouldn't be able to breathe.

Of course, at the time Dean hadn't known that when he finally *did* find her, she would be wrapped around some stranger in a bar.

Once again, he forced the anger down. "Your mother asked me," he said. "She's really worried about you, Whit. And if she knew I found you wandering around a parking lot in the middle of the night, she'd have a very refined hissy fit." He paused. "You have a right to your own life, honey, but surely you can see this is no kind of place for you."

Whitney stared straight ahead, willing herself not to be seduced by the caring in his voice. "What you mean is, Rick's might be all right for someone else, but not for a pampered, *useless* Harcourt brat." She shook her head, annoyed that she was letting the hurt show in her voice. "I'm doing just fine, Dean. Since I've been coming here, you're the only one who's given me any real trouble.

"Whitney."

Whitney didn't look at him, but she felt his gaze on her as he spoke.

"Whitney, I'm sorry...I'm really sorry about the things I said when— That day in my bedroom, you took me by surprise, honey. That's all there is to it."

"I didn't know you needed a warning before you could see me. Do you have to prepare yourself to be nice to me?"

When he hesitated, as though he were having trouble formulating an answer, a tiny, piercing pain went right to the center of her.

"And that kiss just now?" she asked, her voice hard with suppressed emotion. "You can't say I caught you by surprise tonight. And if it was supposed to be some kind of object lesson, I'm afraid you slipped right into overkill."

"Don't you damn well think you could use—" He broke off and drew in a slow breath. When he continued, his voice was calm once again. "No, I wasn't trying to show you what can happen when you don't watch your step. My only excuse is, I was mad as hell. You know what my temper's like."

"I'm beginning to find out," she muttered. "Forget it, Dean. I have. It doesn't matter anymore."

Lies, she told herself sadly, *all lies.* It mattered more than she cared to think about. It mattered more than he would ever know.

She turned and met his eyes. "Since you're here, in Dallas, I assume you know I came here to look for my father." When he nodded, she said, "I found him, Dean. That's why I'm at Rick's. That's why I'm living in this part of town. I want to be close to him. I want to get to know him. I want to let him get to know me."

"The man at your table? Did he recognize you? Does he know who you are?"

"No, not yet. I can't tell him yet." She bit her lip. "It's complicated . . . but the reasons don't really matter. The important thing is, we're building a friendship. We're right on the brink of getting close." She gave her head a little shake. "This is important to me, Dean. I'm not going to give up now."

Dean exhaled a slow breath. It hurt a little that she felt she had to explain how important her father was to her. Hadn't he tried for most of his life to help her cope with Lloyd Grant's absence? Hadn't he held her in his arms when she cried from grief that, although diminishing through the years, never quite left her?

"Okay," he said slowly, "I can see you feel deeply about this. And I'm glad you found your father. You can't doubt that." He glanced at her. "Do you like him, Whit? Is he the way you remembered?"

Whitney had opened her mouth to tell him about the gentle, troubled man she'd found, to explain about the insecurity she felt when she thought about telling Lloyd who she really was, but before the words were fully formed, she swallowed them. She couldn't force Dean back into the role of counselor and confidant. She had to deal with this on her own.

"I like him," she said simply. "He looks different from the man in my memories, and right now we're not much more than casual friends, but I think… Maybe there's some kind of genetic bond, or maybe we're simply on the same wavelength. Whatever it is, I can feel us pulling closer. It's like real affection, true affinity, is just sitting there waiting for us to discover it."

She smiled. "I'm learning to be patient, Dean. That should please you. And in the meantime, I have my job at the factory." Whitney felt more than saw his startled reaction. "Oh, yes," she said with a smile. "I have a real honest-to-goodness job. I use my background in art to get all those little wheels symmetrically arranged on those little toy trucks."

"Assembly line?" The words sounded strangely choked.

"Yup," she said cheerfully. "And I don't want to hear any disparaging remarks. We blue-collar workers are very sensitive to slurs. We take a great deal of pride in what we do. And for your information, I like my work. Very much. I work hard all day, come out here to Rick's to unwind with my friends, then go home to my new apartment to sleep the sleep of the righteous."

"I knew about the apartment," he said slowly. "That's how I found you tonight, but the rest..." His voice faded away, and he leaned forward to rest his chin on the steering wheel. "You'll have to give me a minute to take in the rest of it. An *assembly line,* Whit?"

She laughed. "Believe it or not, I'm getting good at it. Mother would have a stroke if she saw me. I even wear a scarf to keep my hair out of the way. Frankly, I think the peasant look suits me."

After a moment, she turned to meet his eyes in the dim light. "The fact is, my whole life suits me now, Dean. So if you came here to take me back, you'll have to forget it. I'm staying."

A long moment passed before he spoke. "I told your mother that I would let you make your own decisions. I refused to either force or coerce you." His lips twisted in a rueful smile. "It's easy to be unbiased from a distance, but now that I'm here, I find my objectivity is shot to hell. I am biased, Whitney. I might as well admit that up front. And I'm worried about you. You were never taught the coping skills necessary to survive in this kind of place.

She turned away from the affectionate anxiety in his eyes. "You're wrong," she said quietly. "*You* taught me. You taught me to adapt, to handle any new situation that came along. Without flinching. Without complaining." She drew in a slow breath and turned to look at him again. "These people . . . They like me, Dean."

He made a sound of exasperation. "Of course they like you. That was a stupid thing to say."

"Not so stupid." Her lips curved in a small smile. "What I meant was, they like me without knowing I'm a Harcourt. Back home, I was treated with respect, even awe, because of who I was. But here, they respect me for *what* I am. That kind of thing is addictive, Dean." She paused. "I need to stay here and get some answers. I need to know why Daddy left, why he never came back, or even got in touch with me. And I need to know what kind of person he is when I look at him from an adult perspective instead of with the adoration of a little girl. But—and maybe this is the most important thing—I also need to find out what kind of person Whitney Grant is."

She reached out and touched his cheek. "I'm sorry if I caused problems for you. I never wanted to do that." She let her hand fall to her lap. "Go home now,

Dean. And stop worrying about me. I'm fine." She bit her lip. "Tell my mother I'll call her when…when I'm settled in."

He nodded slowly. "If that's what you want," he said finally. After a moment he moved to open the door. "You'll take care?" he asked without looking at her as he stepped from the car.

"Sure," she said, keeping her voice light. "And you do the same."

She slid into the driver's seat and watched Dean walk away, into the darkness, out of her life, then she started the Buick and pulled out of the parking lot.

Fifteen minutes later, when she walked into her apartment, Whitney turned on everything. All the lights, the television and the radio in the kitchen.

It didn't work. The noise and lights didn't even begin to fill the rooms. Although Dean had never been in her apartment, she still felt his absence keenly. And she still had to live goodbye all over again.

When her neighbor to the east began to pound on the wall, Whitney turned everything off, took a shower, and climbed into bed. As she lay on top of the covers, she stared at the ceiling and willed her body to relax. Tonight she wouldn't pull up memories of him, and she wouldn't fantasize about a someday wedding.

But there was no way she could keep from thinking of him, about the way he'd looked tonight. Had he lost weight? She was almost positive there were lines in his face that hadn't been there the last time she saw him. What had he been doing to himself? He probably wasn't eating right.

She shifted restlessly on the bed. Being away from his work must have been hell for him. He shouldn't have done that. He shouldn't have neglected his work to come looking for her.

It would be better for him now, she told herself. Now that they had actually said goodbye face-to-face, now that he had seen for himself that she was making a new life for herself, he would be able to forget about her and get on with his own life.

And, acknowledging how well everything had worked out, Whitney rolled over and cried herself to sleep.

Dean closed his eyes so the redhead in the seat next to him would think he had fallen asleep. He was in no mood to flirt. In fact he was in no mood to be on this plane. Had he given in to his real mood, he would have stayed in Dallas and kicked somebody's butt out of sheer frustration, preferably the muscle-bound imbecile who had been kissing Whitney in that bar.

Get a grip, Dean told himself. Wasn't this just exactly what he'd wanted? He had convinced himself that all he wanted was for Whitney to lose her dependency on him and have a normal life. That was why he had always been so open with her about the women he dated. Hell, it was why he was with the women in the first place, to convince her that she had to let go of her childish obsession for him.

Not that Whitney hadn't had dates. She'd gone out with plenty of boys in high school. Prep-school types. Boys who were destined to have their names bold-faced in the society pages of the newspaper. Young men wearing natural fiber clothes, who came to her stamped with the Harcourt seal of approval.

Whitney had dated them; she had even liked a few. But more often than not, she would come to Dean with a wicked imitation of the way they talked and walked and thought. The few she had liked, she kept as friends. All the others she had ruthlessly discarded, heedless of her mother and uncle's outrage.

When Dean had grown exasperated, waiting for her to form even one romantic attachment, he had become more open with Whitney about the women he dated, trying to show her that he had a personal life, one that didn't include her.

But, true to form, Whitney hadn't reacted as he'd expected her to. There had been no angry confrontations, no bouts of weeping. Although she made a show of jealousy, it was a teasing kind of thing. It was as though she were waiting, as though she knew that one day he would turn to her.

And Dean pretended, even to himself, that her obstinacy made him angry. Tonight he had learned the truth. When he'd seen her in the arms of a stranger, he knew he had been lying to himself.

Turning his head toward the window, he shifted in his seat. Learning the truth about himself was distinctly unpleasant. Disillusioning. He'd believed he was stronger. Now he could see that all along he had been feeding on Whitney's unassuming adoration, using it to sustain himself, to keep his head above water.

No matter what he faced in the courtroom, no matter how many times he got knocked down, no matter what changes occurred in his life, he knew he could count on Whitney to stay the same. He knew she would be there for him, telling him that whatever happened, he would always be her hero. It was the one constant in his life. Whitney's laughing, loving devotion had grounded him.

Opening his eyes, Dean stared out the window at the darkness. Clouds obscured the lights from the towns below and night obscured everything else. He had never liked flying at night. Planes were always smaller at night, the surrounding wall of black isolating. The interior of the plane became the whole world.

He hadn't brought any work with him, which meant there was nothing to keep his mind occupied, nothing to stop the memories.

As he stared into the darkness, the window became a screen onto which his mind projected bits and pieces of the past. Flash cards of days gone by.

There Dean could see the day he'd found her, sitting on the curb, no part of Trash Town but there just the same. And now a picture of Whitney showing him the beaver costume she would wear in her third-grade play. He saw her dressed in riding clothes and a little hard hat, holding up her first riding trophy. He saw her on the night before her first school dance, wearing the poufy pink dress her mother had chosen, the running shoes on her feet spoiling the too adorable look.

And then the scene changed, and Dean saw the first time he'd known that he wanted her.

Drawing in a deep, shaky breath, he closed his eyes against the vision, but it didn't help. It was still there, more vivid than ever.

In the vision he was twenty-four and Whitney was sixteen. Even now, when he was looking at it rather than living it, Dean didn't know why it had happened at that particular moment. There had been no reason or rhyme to it. The jeans and T-shirt she wore were, by no definition of the word, provocative. And there had been nothing flirtatious either in her words or in her attitude.

They had been sitting side by side on the back stoop, close but not touching, as she told him about sneaking out of Sweet House in the middle of the night so she could ride without anyone critiquing her performance on a horse. As she described the moonlight ride, sharing her feelings of exultation when she and the horse flew together across Harcourt land, Dean found himself watching her mouth. And that was when it happened. That was when he knew he wanted her.

At twenty-four, physical needs held no mysteries for Dean. He had been with women. But he had never felt anything as overwhelming as what he felt right then, sitting on the steps beside Whitney.

As she settled back, their bodies overlapped slightly and she leaned comfortably against him. It was the kind of touching that frequently took place in a friendly relationship. Nothing out of the ordinary. No sensual intent behind it. But, God, it felt sensual to Dean. And as she continued to talk, he suddenly realized his hand was resting on her waist. He had no idea how it got there, but now that it was, he couldn't seem to shift it. He felt the heat of her flesh burning into his palms as though the T-shirt were nothing more than a figment of his imagination. And when she moved her head, he felt each separate strand of black hair that brushed across his lips, as though they had taken on a life of their own, deliberately taunting him, willfully seducing him.

As he held her in an almost embrace, every muscle in his body grew hard and tight and hot, and his breath came in labored drafts. He couldn't seem to concentrate on what she was saying. Although he could feel her laughter in the palm of his hand, he had no idea what caused it.

When his hand began to move at her waist, as though his fingers felt an independent need to touch more of her, Dean knew he had to stop it. Jerking abruptly away from her, he forced himself to stand up and move away, his hands shaking, his lungs on fire.

He had spoken sharply to her then, telling her he didn't have time to sit around gossiping, and walking past her into the house, he had closed the door and locked it.

Dean had known Whitney since she was six years old, and their relationship had never been simple. It wasn't merely friendship. And he didn't see her as a little sister. He wasn't sure just how to define the ties that held them together, but he had felt, felt from the very first day, that it was his job to take care of her.

But on that day when she was sixteen, out of the blue he found himself wanting her with an unbelievable urgency. He wanted to take her. He wanted her naked beneath him. He wanted to feel her body moving beneath his. He wanted to taste her, every inch of her.

The sensations were so strong—the scent of her in his nostrils, the taste of her on his tongue—that the very air around him felt electrically charged, as though he had actually felt her naked flesh against his.

Confused and embarrassed, it had taken Dean weeks to get over the experience. And the worst part, the part that haunted his darkest hours, was that Dean knew he could have Whitney. He was her champion, and she made no secret of the fact that she had a crush on him. She was so warm and loving, she would have come to his bed gladly, joyfully.

And sometimes, in the middle of a sleepless night when desperation took hold of him, he considered asking her to do just that. He considered using her misguided, unformed emotions to get what he was so desperately wanted.

He was ashamed that he had even allowed the thought to cross his mind, but shame didn't make the craving for her go away. It was as if his desire had been a tethered demon, and once unleashed, it refused to be contained again.

For most of her life, Whitney had come to Dean for affection ... understanding ... compassion ... companionship. For all the things she didn't get from the Harcourts. And suddenly he was afraid to touch her, afraid his need for her would get out of hand.

He had to tell himself over and over that Whitney was just another pampered Harcourt brat, as different from himself as night from day. There was no place in his life for someone like Whitney. Chance had brought them together, but reality kept them from being anything other than friends. That was the way Dean wanted it, he told himself. A friendship he could handle. Anything else didn't bear thinking about.

Whitney accepted the new restrictions he had placed on their relationship. Without demur, without questions. But although she wasn't as free with her affection as she had been in the past, she flatly refused to let him step out of her life completely. They remained friends, and as the years passed, Dean had learned to control the demon within him. There were times he even thought he had conquered it.

But on the day she left San Antonio, on the day she had walked unannounced into his bedroom, he had been forced to acknowledge the truth. The demon—the overpowering need, the devastating hunger—was still there inside him, waiting to get out and destroy them both.

But in spite of all that, it had all worked out. Dean's strength of purpose, the control he has imposed on his own will, had worked. Whitney was over her infatuation. She had finally recognized the fact that heroes could live only in the rarefied atmosphere of childhood. You couldn't carry them along with you into the adult world.

Whitney was at last making a new life, a real life, for herself. Dean had won.

So why didn't he feel triumphant? he wondered. Why did he feel so damned empty?

Chapter Eight

"I don't understand it," Lloyd said. "How can you be so brilliant at darts and so pitiful at bowling?"

Unaffected by the insult, Whitney held her hands over the air dryer as she waited for her ball to return. "It's very simple. Pick up a dart, then try picking up one of these bowling balls. 'You canna change the laws of physics, Captain Kirk.' It has something to do with thrust and force and expendable energy."

"And that's why the ball lands in the gutter every time?" Lloyd asked.

"She's conning you," Frankie called from the next lane. "Face it, Mary, you stink like a big dog. You're the only person in the history of bowling to come up with a negative score."

Frankie's opinion and her digital response brought a roar of raucous laughter from the group, but Whitney ignored them and picked up her ball. She went carefully through the steps that Lloyd had taught her—hold the ball at chest level; step and thrust out; step and swing back; step and release on the return swing—then she sighed heavily as the ball headed straight for the gutter.

After curtsying to the burst of enthusiastic applause—people she didn't even know were keeping track of her score—Whitney headed for the ladies' room to freshen up.

She was washing her hands when a petite, attractive blonde came out of one of the stalls. Linelle Pierce also worked at the toy factory, but since she had an office job, Whitney didn't see her as often as she did the rest of the group.

"I'm glad you don't let their teasing bother you," Linelle said as she fussed with her hair. "They all like you a lot. Especially Frankie."

Whitney studied the blonde's carefully composed features. "Do I detect a hidden question there? Like, am I interested in Mr. Watch-Me-Flex-My-Muscles Halloran?" Whitney grinned. "You don't have to worry about me, Linelle. Frankie is right out of my league. I would never aspire so high."

"Somehow I get the feeling Frankie wouldn't agree with you," the woman said gloomily.

Whitney took a lipstick out of her purse. "Frankie simply likes a challenge. If I were really hot for him, he wouldn't give me the time of day. Next time you're talking to him, let your attention wander off to another man. Just see what kind of reaction you get then.'' She grinned. "If he doesn't strain a tendon trying to impress you, I'll eat my bowling shoes.''

After a moment of thought Linelle gave a slow smile. "Why not? I couldn't be worse off, that's for sure.''

As she watched Whitney apply her lipstick, the blonde's expression grew thoughtful, and after a moment she dropped her gaze to her hands. "Mary— Look, we don't know each other all that well, and you can tell me to mind my own business if you want, but...'' She raised her head and met Whitney's eyes. "You're not thinking about going after *Lloyd?*''

Whitney choked back startled laughter. "No... really,'' she said, shaking her head vehemently. "It's nothing like that. Lloyd and I are friends. Just friends.''

Linelle relaxed. "That's a relief. I like you, and I like Lloyd. But the two of you *together?* Know what I mean?''

"Is anyone else thinking along those lines?'' Whitney asked with a worried frown. "Do the rest of the gang think that Lloyd and I are, you know... *together?*''

The blonde shrugged. "A few of them, maybe. I mean, you spend all your time hanging around Lloyd, and as far as we know, you haven't had a single date since you started out at the factory. Lloyd told them nothing was going on between the two of you, but you know how men are. They just wouldn't let it alone.''

"Lloyd told them—" She broke off and shook her head. "He didn't say a word. Why didn't he tell me the guys were razzing him?"

"Maybe he was embarrassed. You know how *private* Lloyd is." Linelle paused. "If you haven't got a thing for Lloyd, then how come you don't ever date? There are plenty of guys at the factory, not all of them slugs, either, who would jump at the chance to go out with you. Say, I could fix you up if you want. Maybe we could double."

"That's really sweet of you, Linelle, but I don't think so. I'm just not ready yet."

"Yet?" Linelle narrowed her eyes at Whitney, giving her an ah-ha look. "I thought so. You're coming down from a bad man trip. Am I right?"

"Something like that."

"Hey, forget him. Men are worms." The blonde leaned back against the vanity counter. "Have you ever looked at a night crawler up close?"

"Noo-oo," Whitney said slowly. "I can't say that I have."

"Try it sometime. Get two of them and see if you can tell any difference. It's impossible. One might be longer or shorter than the other—you can take that any way you like—" she added with a grin "—but they're basically the same. You gave me some advice, so now I'm going to return the favor. It's stupid to let yourself get all messed up over one worm when you can dig up another one just like it."

"Pithy," Whitney said, nodding judicially. "Really pithy. The only flaw I see in your hypothesis is a muscle-bound wonder named Frankie."

Linelle laughed and shook her head. "I was afraid you'd remember him. Okay, so I don't believe a word of what I just said. And apparently, neither do you."

"No." Whitney smiled. "Because my night crawler wasn't a duplicate of anything. You could line up a thousand earthworms beside him, and I'd still know the difference. Instantly and without a doubt."

As though she had seen something in Whitney's eyes, Linelle put a sympathetic hand on her shoulder. "I'm sorry, honey. Sometimes it works out that way, damn their eyes."

Whitney shrugged. She knew Linelle wanted to hear the details of her "bad man trip," but Whitney wasn't willing to have her relationship with Dean turned into just another affair gone wrong. She wouldn't ever be able to talk about it with the casual but enthusiastic indignation with which most women treated their past love affairs.

Turning toward the door, she smiled again and said, "I hope you'll have better luck with Frankie."

After playing another game the party began to break up, and it was just after three when Whitney followed Lloyd out of the bowling alley to his station wagon.

She and Lloyd still took separate cars to work, but occasionally on the weekends, if the gang from the factory was getting together at the lake or the bowling alley, she and Lloyd would ride together. It was a small step, but she figured a small step was better than no step at all.

Linelle had been right when she said Lloyd was a private person, and Whitney disliked knowing that their friendship was causing him problems, but she couldn't back off now. She simply couldn't.

In the two weeks since Dean's sudden appearance, Lloyd had gradually begun to grow more comfortable in her presence. There were even times when he seemed glad to see her, which was fortunate, because Whitney made sure he saw her as often as possible. He laughed more often now, and what was even more important, his laughter no longer took him by surprise. Maybe it was wishful thinking on her part, but it seemed that he was coming back to life a little more each day.

And not before time, she told herself as he parked the station wagon in his regular space at the side of their apartment building.

Garden Court Apartments was a small complex that consisted of four separate, two-story buildings that were arranged around a central courtyard. The Court contained no indoor corridors; the apartments all opened onto covered walkways that overlooked the courtyard.

Lloyd's apartment was on the upper level of the west unit and, with some careful maneuvering, Whitney had managed to get one just three doors away.

"I don't know what you keep going on about," she said once they reached his door. "I took out six pins in that last game. That's definitely progress."

"You might say that," he said, nodding sagely. "But you'd be the only one. I probably should have explained that the object of the game is to try and knock over the pins in your *own* lane."

"I was hoping you hadn't noticed that," she said, her voice peevish.

As she stood watching Lloyd laugh at her expense, Whitney moved out of the way so that a man with a large cardboard box could pass by them. Out of the corner of her eyes she saw the newcomer stop in front of an apartment four doors down, just on the far side of Whitney's.

When the man put down the box and inserted a key in the door, Whitney frowned. Something about him was beginning to nag at her. She turned her head for a better look and instantly drew in a sharp breath, her eyes widening in shock.

The new tenant wore a gray sweatshirt with the sleeves cut out, and his faded jeans fit like a glove across well-shaped buttocks. Even though the man had his back turned to her, Whitney recognized him now.

Oh yes, she knew that backside.

Dean turned and nodded his head in greeting. "How're you doing?" he said, his smile polite, his dark eyes gleaming with suppressed laughter.

"Mary?"

Whitney turned to find Lloyd watching her, making no effort to hide his amusement. "Are you going to introduce me to your friend?" Lloyd asked.

Leaving the box on the walkway, Dean walked back to where they stood. "Yes, Mary, introduce us."

She was going to kill him. She was going to kill him in a way that was painful. And slow.

After sending Dean a vengeful look, she said, "Lloyd, this is Dean Russell . . . an old friend. Dean, Lloyd Grant."

"A new friend," Lloyd said as he shook Dean's hand.

Whitney stood a step away from the two men, feeling anger and a lot of other things she didn't want to think about at the moment. She wanted to concentrate on the anger. At least until she found out what in hell was going on.

"The apartment only became available yesterday," Dean was telling Lloyd. "I was really lucky to get it. Fortunately the manager thought I had a trustworthy look about me."

Enough was enough. Grasping Dean's arm tightly, Whitney began walking back toward the door that he had left open.

"Dean, dear, you probably need some help getting unpacked. You should have let me know you were moving in today. You know how *helpful* I can be." She glanced over her shoulder. "See you tonight, Lloyd."

"Yeah . . . see you tonight, Lloyd," Dean called.

When they were both inside his apartment—*his apartment*—Whitney slammed the door behind them and looked him over slowly and carefully.

The way he was dressed reminded her of the way he used to look back when he was that wild boy from

Trash Town. A little uncivilized and totally sensual. He also looked as though he were laughing at a secret joke, as if he were thoroughly enjoying her anger, damn his sexy eyes.

"What in hell do you think you're doing?" she burst out, her voice high with incredulity. "Why are you here? What about your practice? If you mess this up for me, Dean, so help me God, I'll never forgive you."

Dean threw back his head and laughed. Sweet heaven, it was good to see her again.

"Let's take those in order," he said. "Your first question, I believe, was what in hell do I think I'm doing here? That's easy—I'm moving in. Second, why am I here? Because for good or for bad, and no matter what I've said to make you think otherwise, I made myself responsible for you eighteen years ago. I can't let go until I know you're okay. What I saw last time I was here didn't convince me of that. The third question was, what about my practice? I turned most of my cases over to Sam. The rest I'll handle from here, flying back to San Antonio when I need to."

What he didn't tell her was that the past two weeks had been pure, unadulterated hell, first making the decision to come here, then arranging to handle, on a commuter basis, the cases he couldn't turn over to Sam.

"And as for the last question," he continued. "But that wasn't a question, was it? It was an assumption that would probably offend me if I were in the mood to be offended, which I'm not." He met her eyes. "I have no intention of messing this up for you. I think you should get to know your father. When have I ever wanted less than the best for you, Whitney?''

Whitney turned away from him. Damn it, she didn't want to love him. Why couldn't she stop? Why couldn't she stay mad? It wasn't right that he could walk in, say a few words, and have her melting inside all over again.

"It just seems like you're going a little overboard," she said, her uncertainty showing in her voice. "I knew you felt responsible for me, but this is too much, Dean. Why should you neglect your own life just to make sure mine is going well?" She shook her head slowly. "I don't like it. I've never asked this kind of thing of you."

"I know you didn't." She heard him move, then his voice came from directly behind her. "You never asked anything of me. This is for *me*, Whitney. Strictly for me. Okay?"

She turned to face him, examining his eyes. She could always see the truth in his eyes. "Okay," she said after a moment.

He picked up her hands and gave them both a slight squeeze. "That's better."

This was going to take some mental adjustment, Whitney told herself as she casually pulled her hands free. Dean was in her life again, and she wasn't sure how she felt about that. She wasn't sure how he *wanted* her to feel about it.

For most of her life Whitney had chased Dean, and Dean had done his level best to hold her off. She didn't know how to react to this obvious reversal of roles. Who was she supposed to be now? What was she supposed to be to Dean? Had all the rules changed, or only some of them?

There was an awkwardness, an awareness, between them that had never been there in the past, and that was what she was going to have to learn to deal with.

The situation needed thought. A *lot* of thought. But that would have to come later. Maybe later, when she wasn't thrown into turmoil by his presence, she would be able to think more clearly.

"The Gutierrez case," she said suddenly. "That was important to you. How can you leave it to Sam? That boy was counting on you."

He smiled. "Alvo's fine. I had it all but wrapped up before you did your disappearing act."

"Really?" She was surprised and pleased, for Dean and for the boy. "How did you pull it off?"

"I didn't. Tess gets all the credit."

Twenty minutes later they were sitting on cardboard cartons, while he finished telling her about what had really happened to Alvo Gutierrez. As she listened, Whitney's blue eyes grew sad, her natural empathy tuned to a couple of children she had never met.

"What's going to happen to them now?" she asked.

"We'll be lucky if Jackson gets six months."

She made a disgusted sound. "That stinks, Dean. That really stinks."

"I know," he agreed, "but at least it's a breathing space. The three of them—Alvo, Tess and their mother—are in counseling and—"

"How did you manage that? I thought the mother was obsessing on her husband? How did you get her to consider her children for once?"

"You'd be surprised what a little unofficial visit from the district attorney's office will do. I asked a friend to call on Mrs. Jackson and suggest that she could possibly be charged with aiding and abetting... unless she decided to get help for herself and the kids. By the time Jackson gets out, Alvo and Tess—if not their mother—will be stronger. Now they know that they have someone on their side. If trouble starts again, they know they can call the authorities. And maybe, if everything works out—and if I have anything to say about it, it will—they won't ever accept abuse as a normal way of life again."

He stared out the window. "Alvo's got a lot of anger to work out, Whit. And the anger that's most damaging to him emotionally isn't what he feels for his stepfather. It's all the hidden stuff he feels for his mother. He doesn't know it yet, but he blames her. He blames her for having the bad judgment to marry that worthless sleaze in the first place. And he blames her for not protecting him. Alvo thinks he's an adult, an adult who understands all about human weakness, but inside there's still a child who thinks parents are supposed to be all-powerful and all-wise. Strong enough and smart enough to keep the bad things away."

He exhaled slowly, his strong lips twisting in a self-mocking smile. "And of course there's always that little demon inside him that keeps telling Alvo that he got just exactly what he deserved."

As Dean spoke the quiet, unemotional words, Whitney felt an old familiar pain well up inside her. Alvo's story was too close to what had happened to Dean all those years ago. And as always, she wanted so badly to hold him, to rock him until the past let go of him.

Instead she cleared her throat. "You're a good man, Dean Russell," she said, her voice husky. "A good, kind, caring man. No, don't shake your head. And don't tell me you were only doing your job. You saved those kids."

Grinning, he drew back his head to look at her. "One man against the forces of evil? I feel like I should be standing on top of a building, my hands on my hips while my cape blows in the wind."

"As a matter of fact I've always thought you would look pretty darn cute in tights."

He chuckled, and after a moment he stood up and moved away to pick up the box he had just inside the front door. After placing it on the table, he called back to her, "So what are we doing tonight?"

"We're playing penny-ante poker at my place." She walked to the door and opened it. "Eight o'clock. Don't be late."

"Hey, I thought you were going to help me unpack."

She looked over her shoulder and raised one slender brow. "Do I look like a Mayflower man?" she asked as she walked out the door.

Back in her apartment, Whitney took a quick shower and barely had time to get into yellow shorts and a matching cotton knit shirt before she heard a knock on her front door.

"I'm coming! Hold on a second," she yelled, scrambling into white sandals on her way to the door. Before the game, she and Lloyd had decided to try a little Mexican restaurant that everyone at work had been talking about.

Throwing open the door, she said, "Listen, Lloyd, I've been—" The words died away when she saw Dean standing behind her father.

"Look who I ran into," Lloyd said, his grin matching Dean's. "He was wandering around looking hungry, so I invited him to come along with us. Since you two are old friends, I knew you wouldn't mind."

"Hello, Mary," Dean said. "Where are we going to eat?"

Whitney had been wondering how Dean and Lloyd would get along. Now she knew. They looked like two little boys bent on devilish deeds.

Lloyd's acceptance—which grew even more apparent over dinner—didn't mean the rest of the group from the factory would follow suit. Although they were in no way a hostile bunch, they always stood back a little from newcomers, as if they were waiting for some secret signal that this person wasn't going to throw a kink into the well-oiled machinery of the group.

Whitney had invited five of her new friends to the poker game at her house. With Lloyd, Dean and herself, that made eight in the game. Along with four metal dining chairs, a stepladder, footstool, vanity stool and armchair from the living room were crowded around her little Formica dining table.

There was a lot of elbow clashing, and the drinks, dip and chips—the edible variety—that cluttered the table didn't leave much room for poker, but no one seemed to notice.

Dean kept quiet at first, letting her friends get used to his presence, then gradually he began to join in their easy, joking banter. The fact that he took his wins and losses with the same casual good humor was a big plus.

Luckily no one recognized Dean as the man in the expensive suit who had briefly stepped into Rick's Pub one night. Following Lloyd's advice, Dean had decided he wouldn't tell Whitney's friends that he was a practicing attorney. Lawyers, even those of the ambulance-chasing breed, didn't live in this part of town. Because it went against the grain to tell an outright lie, he simply told them he worked in a building that housed a lot of hotshot lawyers, and when the word maintenance was casually thrown into the conversation, they were left with the impression that Dean was a janitor.

For her part, Whitney hadn't doubted for a moment that her co-workers would like Dean. She had, however, expected them to hold back for a while, the way they had done with her. But after she had won her third hand in a row, she realized that somehow Dean had already become a part of the group.

She had promised herself she would try to duplicate Dean's casual attitude toward winning, but after
taking the pot three times in a row, she raked in the
large pile of pennies, singing under her breath, "I'm
bad . . . I'm bad."

Dean picked up a tortilla chip, leaned back in his
chair and studied the triangular chip carefully. After
a moment he ran his gaze around the table.

"One...two...three," he said quietly, and the next
thing Whitney knew, she was dodging the tortilla chips
that flew at her from every direction.

She should have known Dean would fit in. It wasn't
only that he knew what it was like to struggle to survive or that he spoke their language. Dean simply had
a way of connecting with people.

" . . . So I thought maybe she would behave herself
for a little while, but no such luck," Dean told Lloyd.
"It wasn't a week later that she blew up the kitchen."

"You know good and well that wasn't my fault,"
Whitney protested.

After the gang from the factory left, Dean, Whitney and Lloyd had moved the party to Dean's apartment so that he could share his record collection with
Lloyd, but the music was forgotten when the older
man began to question Dean about his friend Mary.

"I was simply trying to feed a stray cat," Whitney
continued, her voice righteous. "Besides, I was only
seven. How would I know how a kitchen works?"

Dean leaned towards Lloyd. "She thought maybe
the cat would like a hot meal, so she stuck a jar of

spaghetti sauce in the oven and turned the sucker on full blast. Then she promptly forgot all about it."

Whitney smiled in spite of herself. "He looked like an old American sort of cat, so I decided that he would rather have a hot dog."

"The explosion was heard 'round the world," Dean said. "I didn't ever go to her house, but when she told me about it, I couldn't resist. I snuck around back and looked in the kitchen window. The oven door was swinging on one hinge and spaghetti sauce was everywhere. Splattered all over the ceiling and walls. It looked like a madman with a chainsaw had been turned loose in a slaughterhouse."

Whitney glared at the two men who were doubled over with laughter. "I hope you both choke," she muttered, then after a moment, she frowned down at her coffee. "Speaking of choking, I think I better trade this for seltzer."

Dean wiped his eyes and groaned. "I was wondering when somebody was going to mention our dinner. That had to be the worst stuff I've ever eaten. Either we went on an off night or everyone at the factory has the taste buds of a doorknob."

"There's something about burnt chili peppers that lingers on the tongue and in the mind," Whitney said with an expressive grimace.

Grinning, Dean stood up and moved toward the kitchen. "I'll pour us all a glass of milk...unless anyone would rather have ipecac?"

As soon as Dean was out of the room, Whitney turned her attention back to Lloyd. "Why do you encourage him to tell those stupid stories?'' she asked in exasperation. ''I expected your eyes to start glazing over about five minutes after he went off on this excursion into yesteryear, but you just kept on saying 'More, more.'''

Smiling, he shook his head. ''I enjoy his Little Mary stories. And he obviously enjoys telling them.''

''Sure he does,'' she agreed, her voice dry. ''They're all at my expense. He likes to see me squirm.'' She drew her knees up beside her on the couch. ''Turnabout's fair play. Tell me a Little Lloyd story. Do you have brothers and sisters? A big family?''

He shook his head. ''There was a brother, but he died several years before I was born.''

''I'm sorry.''

Lloyd's eyes grew a little sadder. ''I didn't know him, so I could only mourn an idea. I'm sure the loss was rough on my mother and father—that's the worst thing that can happen to a parent—but James was never real to me.''

Slowly, almost reluctantly, he began to tell her about his childhood, about growing up in a small town in Illinois. Since both his parents worked, he'd spent a good deal of his time alone, but he hadn't minded. He had things to occupy his mind, things to dream about.

On summer days, when school had let out for the year, he would turn to the railroad track that ran behind his house and follow it for miles. He had a notion that something—adventure, life, *something*—was out there, waiting for him, if he could just walk far enough.

"Every child thinks he will be something great, something important," he said with a twisted little smile. "That's probably what mid-life crisis is all about. You wake up one day, half your life is over, and you discover that you're nothing more than an ordinary man, that you'll never live up to your childhood dreams."

She was silent for a moment, caught up in his recollections. "What was your dream?" she asked finally.

He smiled. "I was going to be a world-famous paleontologist. The next Louis Leakey. The dream was still alive in college, probably because I didn't have a lot of close friends who could influence me with more prosaic, more profitable dreams," he acknowledged.

After a moment of silence he shook his head, as though to clear away the visions. "Colleges are the world's storehouses for possibilities. All kinds of wonderful things, a multitude of dreams, are laid out before you, like offerings to an ancient king. You start out pursuing them with all your heart, but somehow, somewhere along the way, the dreams change."

He rubbed his face slowly, as though he were growing tired. "It's probably a physiological thing. Maturity...hormones...the need for security. Who knows? You simply wake up one day and realize the dreams have become a person. There is someone in your life who makes you more than you were before. There is a star that shines only for you. Someone who makes waking up in the morning an extraordinary event."

He shifted restlessly. "Your center of attention shifts. All your energy...all your *passion* is given over to an individual rather than an idea. The great and important things you dreamed about when you were a child seem like nothing more than flights of fancy."

"Is that the way it happened to you?" she asked, struggling to keep the intensity out of her voice. "Did you find the star that shined only for you?"

As she watched him, she caught a glimpse of intense, personal pain. Then he closed his eyes, and when he opened them again, the wall was up, shutting her out.

A slight noise penetrated her disappointment and she glanced up to find Dean standing in the doorway of the kitchen. In his dark eyes was a look of sympathy that encompassed both of the people in his living room.

A quarter of an hour later, after Lloyd had made his excuses and left, Whitney leaned her head against the back of the couch and exhaled a slow breath.

"It hurts every time," she said softly. "Every time I see him shut himself behind that wall, it hurts. And the thing is, I'm not sure whether I'm feeling his pain or my own." She shook her head in a weary movement. "When I first came here I was afraid to tell him that I was his daughter because— You see, I wasn't sure that after nineteen years he would even remember that he had a daughter once. But I'd forgotten about the letters." She glanced up at him. "Did Mother tell you about the letters?"

"Not directly. I gather she burned them."

She nodded. "It wasn't a small pile of ashes, Dean. He must have written often over the years. And if the one I found in her desk was anything like the others, he didn't forget. He didn't forget her and he didn't forget me. He still loved me in that letter."

"So what's stopping you from telling him now?"

"You saw him pull back tonight. Anytime I even get close to mentioning his past, he does that. How do you think he'll react when he realizes he's looking his past in the face? Maybe I'm making a mistake, but I'm hoping that if he comes to see me as a friend first, a real friend, he won't run from me."

He dropped down beside her and put his arm around her, pulling her close for a moment in a semi-hug. "I'm sorry, Whit. I know it's rough on you. But speaking as an observer, I think you're making progress."

"Maybe. I don't know. It's all so complicated."

"Does that surprise you? All human relationships are complicated. It's the nature of the beast."

She turned her head and slowly examined his face. "Yes," she said slowly. "I guess I knew that already."

When she was a child it had all been so simple. So easy. A thing was either good or bad, with nothing in between. A person was either a friend or an enemy. Relationships were effortless then. For a friend, you held nothing back. You put up no defenses.

Years ago, before she knew how easy it was to get hurt, she and Dean had that kind of uncomplicated relationship. She had always known where she stood.

She'd never had to consider what she said or did. She'd never had to pretend.

But those days were past, she told herself with regret. Nothing would ever be that simple again.

Reaching out, he rested his hand gently on the curves of her cheek. "Are you ever going to forgive me for the things I said to you?"

She met his eyes. "You think I'm holding a grudge?" she asked in quiet surprise. "You don't really know me at all, do you?"

He looked as though the question hurt and after a moment he gave his head a slight shake. "I thought I did. No, I *did*. I did know you, but somewhere along the way you started closing me out. You hid part of yourself from me."

"I closed *you* out?" If it hadn't been so sad, she would have laughed. "The only part I hid was the part you didn't want to see. You wanted me to be a pal...no, don't try to deny it. You wanted someone to relax with, someone to laugh with, so that's who I became. I wasn't pretending. Part of me is like that. In all...friendships...there are adjustments to make. I was one person with you, another with the men I dated and someone completely different for my friends at S.M.U. That's the way it works. Everyone does it. Even you. For me, you were the tolerant big brother. And don't try to tell me you were the same person with Sam or that judge you play golf with."

Dean frowned. The explanation wasn't something he wanted to hear. He didn't like being compared to her casual friends. What they had was more than that. Much more. They were a part of each other.

"Have you grown out of me?" He slid a thumb across her lower lip, tugging at the tender, sensitive flesh. "I didn't want that to happen."

Whitney closed her eyes, fighting to keep from moving closer to him, fighting against the fire burning white-hot inside her.

A year ago she could have accepted Dean's touch as a natural part of life. She hadn't taken him for granted, yet being with him had felt comfortable. It had felt absolutely right. And now a wave of deep regret washed over her as she realized, once again, that it was all gone. All that was left was a nostalgic longing for what had been, what would never be again.

The change hadn't been brought on by her determination to build a life that wasn't centered around him. Change happened on the day she had touched him and allowed him to see the fires burning inside her. She had brought a new element into the equation of Dean and Whitney—sexual awareness. It was Whitney's open, physical need for Dean that had created the uneasiness, the fine tension, that even now filled the space between them. As long as she had kept her desire hidden from him, they had both been able to keep up the pretense that they were the world's best buddies and nothing more.

That day in his bedroom Whitney had given no thought to the consequences. If she'd had her way, they would have made love right then, thereby adding something new to their relationship. But because Dean had wants and needs of his own, desires that were completely different from Whitney's, instead of something being added, something had been taken away.

And only now, as she watched him struggling to retrieve the past, did Whitney feel the full of weight of her loss.

She couldn't change what had happened. She couldn't relive the past, and she could no longer dream about that magical Someday when she could be Dean's forever love. The only choice left to her was to accept reality. And in reality, she and Dean were friends. Old, tried-and-true friends. Nothing more, nothing less.

She opened her eyes. "I'll never outgrow you," she said softly. "But friendships are dynamic things. They grow and change, they evolve. I want you to be a part of my life. Always. But I won't latch onto you anymore. I won't be like an orchid on a tree, with no roots of my own, making do with second-hand stability. We can't go back, Dean. So let's not even try. Let's move on to the next step, explore the hidden parts, the new parts, of each other."

She moved away from him, rising to her feet. "And if we don't like what we find, then maybe what we had wasn't as strong as we thought it was."

"No." The word was low and tight, vehement, and he was on his feet, his hands on her arms. "We weren't wrong. It's strong, Whitney. It's *real*." He made a visible effort to pull himself together, and smiling, he gave her a little shake. "Best friends, right? No matter what."

He needed something from her, some kind of confirmation. She could see it in his eyes, in his too tense smile. "Best friends," she echoed in a whisper. "No matter what."

Chapter Nine

When Whitney spotted a limb in her path, she didn't miss a beat. She jumped over it and kept on jogging.

It was after six and the sun was dipping low in the west. It was a hot day in May, but a slight breeze helped cool the perspiration that dampened her tank top and the waistband of her running shorts.

Thank heaven for sweat, she thought as she glanced at her watch to see how long she had been jogging.

Whitney wanted to wonder where Dean was this evening, but she had already wondered about that twice since she started jogging, and her new rule was that she could only think about him twice in any given hour.

Not thinking about him was only one of the new rules she had written for her life, most of them concerning Dean. On the nights she didn't go to Rick's or get together with Lloyd, Whitney stayed at home. Instead of calling Dean or knocking on his apartment door, she watched television or read or washed clothes, telling herself that, someday, not depending on him wouldn't require as much self-restraint. Someday she wouldn't feel the urgent need to share every minute of her day with him. Someday she wouldn't feel only partially complete when she wasn't with him.

But someday felt a long way away, especially when Dean began dropping by her apartment unannounced, to borrow paper towels, or to tell her about a new development in one of the cases he was working on, or simply to ask how many little tires she had stuck on little trucks at the factory that day. More often than not he would stay to watch television or talk, and before Whitney knew what was happening, they had spent the whole evening together.

Occasionally Whitney managed to think of an excuse for being alone—she was tired or had a headache or was in a tearing PMS rage. But most of the time she wasn't that strong. Just being in the same room with him added more to her life than she was willing to admit.

And sometimes dreams simply refused to die.

Give it a rest, for heaven's sake, she told herself as she negotiated an S-curve in the path.

She had been coming to the little park for a couple of weeks now and her time was getting steadily better.

Every time she ran she managed to cover the three-mile course in a little less time.

Me and Zola Budd, she thought with a grin.

Whitney wasn't trying to run off an excess of energy; she wasn't running in an attempt to deal with sexual frustration, although heaven knew she would take any help she could get in that department. She was running because, after a month of standing in one spot at the factory, she was afraid that everything she ate was going to slide to her ankles. And since none of her new friends kept horses or belonged to a gym, she had sought out this little park two miles from Garden Court.

She was concentrating on keeping her breathing regular when another runner reached her. Barely noticing, she waited for him to pass, but instead he began to keep pace with her. When she dropped back, he dropped back. When she picked up her speed, he followed suit.

Seconds later she stopped abruptly and bent over, her head hanging loosely, her hands on her knees to support her upper body as she drew in short, painful breaths of air.

After a moment she raised her head to look at Dean, her hands still on her knees. He wore his ratty old cutoffs, track shoes and nothing else.

Whitney dropped her head again. Looking at him was a bad move. She definitely wasn't going to cool off or catch her breath that way.

"Are you following me?" she asked finally, her voice rough from exertion.

"I am," he admitted readily as he jogged in place. "But so is that thin guy and the one with the Regis Philbin hair. They're waiting for you to notice them. I, on the other hand, have never believed in being subtle."

She gave a breathless little laugh. "You're an idiot. I had my best time going until you came along." Eyeing him enviously as he continued to jog in place, she muttered, "Show-off."

Spotting runners behind them, she moved off the trail so that the two men could pass. One of them, a thin man, shot a look at Dean before they moved out of sight.

"Eat your heart out," Dean said with an evil grin, then moved over to lean against a tree. "They're obviously not Gilbert and Sullivan fans." At her inquisitive look, he added, "*The Yeomen of the Guard.* You know, 'faint heart never won fair lady' and 'none but the brave deserve the fair.' I think they threw every cliché known to man into that song."

She shook her head. "That's incredible. No, really, it is. I don't think I know another man who goes to Gilbert and Sullivan for advice on how to meet women. And I certainly don't know any men who would admit to it, even if they did. Is this how you got Barbara hooked? Serenading her with 'Titwillow' and 'Three Little Maids'?"

He examined her with a cool look. "You keep this up and you won't have to worry about your running time."

"Why's that?"

"Because I'll be behind you chunking rocks."

Her laugh was slightly stiff. She wanted to ask him if he saw Barbara on his trips back home—he had flown to San Antonio four times in the past three weeks—but she firmly quashed the urge.

Turning her head, she stared at the path ahead. "Only half a mile more. I can make that. Easy. Sure I can. Okay, not easy, but I can still make it. I've got fortitude. Strength of purpose. True grit."

With a little moan, she drew in a deep breath and was about to start out again when he caught her arm. "Are you going to Rick's tonight?"

She shook her head. "No, Lloyd has a cold, so I thought I would stay home. There's a slasher movie on television that I missed when it was in the theaters. You know how I love snuggling up on soft cushions, cocoa and popcorn in hand, while I watch innocent people being disemboweled."

He chuckled. "You're still trying to get back at your mother for not letting you see *Poltergeist* all those years ago."

She glanced away from him. "I don't think I'm ready to think about Mother yet," she said slowly.

With a determined effort, she shook away the feelings. "Gotta run. See ya," she called over her shoulder as she started down the trail again.

Dean didn't catch up with her this time. Whitney knew he could have easily enough. But he didn't. She should have felt some small satisfaction for having successfully put him off. She should have, but she didn't.

After returning to her apartment, Whitney showered and changed into a striped silk caftan, then she ate the salad she had picked up at a local café—she still wasn't much good in a kitchen. It was almost eight when she began arranging her nest. Cushions and afghan on the floor in front of the television. Cocoa on the right, popcorn on the left.

The movie had just been announced when there was a knock on her door.

Stop it, she told herself as her heart jumped in response to the sound. Her heart jumped because even before she opened the door, she knew that it was Dean.

He grinned as he leaned against the doorjamb. "I had a sudden craving for cocoa, popcorn and horror movies. I can't figure it out. It came over me all of a sudden." He moved past her into the room. "Besides, you know you always watch these things with your hands over your eyes. You need someone to tell you when the gory parts are over."

Whitney wasn't going to say a word. She was too lazy, too comfortable to fight him tonight. And after all, he was right. She needed him.

When he reached the couch he stopped to take off his shoes, then, without consulting her, he rearranged the cushions on the floor to accommodate two.

"This movie we're watching," he said as he patted the floor beside him in an invitation for her to sit down, "is it the one where every time the hero stumbles across a bloody body he gazes up at the moon and says, 'He is evil and he must be destroyed'?"

With only the smallest of hesitations, Whitney joined him on the floor. "How should I know? I told you I haven't seen it. So don't even think about spoiling the ending for me."

He snorted. "How can you spoil a slasher movie? They're all exactly the same. This really ugly, really unimaginative dude systematically splatters the blood of a bunch of really cute, really stupid teenagers, and everybody dies except for the girl with the best looking body and the guy with the best looking hair."

She threw a handful of popcorn at him. "You are evil and you must be destroyed."

"Where's my cocoa?" he asked, calmly picking popcorn out of his hair. "Is this how you treat all your guests?" Then, as she walked into the kitchen, he called, "How come I haven't heard you talking about the company picnic? Lloyd says everyone's looking forward to it."

Lloyd says too damn much, she thought with a slight frown. Dean and her father had taken to each other immediately and now it seemed like every time Whitney saw one of them, she saw the other, as well.

"It's no big deal," she called to Dean. "The big shots at the factory are springing for some fried chicken and potato salad, then we all get together at the lake and build goodwill and company camaraderie by trying to annihilate each other at baseball and volleyball and horseshoes . . . that kind of thing."

"Baseball?" he said when she handed him a cup of cocoa. "You're pretty good at that. You might just be able to redeem your reputation. You know, let them all know that there are certain kinds of balls that you can manage to send in the right direction.''

"Somebody's been talking," she said grimly. "Is it my fault you never took me bowling?''

He laughed. "Don't worry. You can show them your stuff when you get a bat in your hand.''

Whitney took a sip of cocoa, watching him from the corners of her eyes. It almost sounded as though he were hinting for an invitation to the picnic. It would certainly make the day more interesting for her. And really, it was only a picnic. What would it hurt if—

She broke off the thought with a little shake of her head. She couldn't keep doing this. For her sake, and for his, she had to show him that she could make it on her own.

"It'll probably rain," she said with an indifferent shrug. "And to tell you the truth, it wouldn't disappoint me all that much if it did. The only reason I'm going is so I can spend more time with Lloyd.''

She could feel his eyes on her, but she didn't look up. Staring at the television, she said, "There's that music. It must be time for the first murder. You'd think these people would catch on. If I were there, as soon as I heard that music, I'd run.''

Accepting the change of subject with a slight smile, Dean settled back against the couch and began to watch the movie with her.

He was right: the movie was a cheap copy of a dozen other horror movies. But that didn't make it any less bloody, any less terrifying.

Half an hour later Whitney said from behind her hands, "Tell me when he gets through killing her."

Dean laughed. "He hasn't even started yet. She's still walking up the stairs. Now she's turning onto the landing. Now she's— Oops, there he goes. Again. And again. And again. And—"

Whitney doubled up her fist and hit him twice, her eyes still closed. "Stop it. You know I can't stand it when— What's happening now?"

"She's dragging herself toward the telephone, showing a little bit of shapely thigh there. Titillation in the midst of destruction. Okay, you can open your eyes now. I think she's gasped her last."

Shuddering, Whitney stood up and walked into the kitchen to put the empty popcorn bowl in the sink. "How can you be so callous? The woman *died.*"

"It's only a movie. And it wasn't even particularly well-done. I don't have any practical experience, but I'm pretty sure you wouldn't say 'Ooh...ooh...aah' while some maniac is hacking at you with a meat cleaver. She didn't even gurgle when he got her in the throat."

"Will you cut it out?" she said in exasperation as she glanced over her shoulder into the living room.

An hour later the movie was over at last. Whitney had been sitting with her back resting against the couch, the afghan pulled up to her nose so that she could hide under it if the need arose.

Now, throwing the afghan aside in disgust, she said, "What a rip-off. There is no way you can kill an adult male by tying a plastic garbage bag over his head . . . because no matter what they say on the commercials, those things are *not* that strong. For heaven's sake, his teeth were a foot long. We saw him rip through a Boy Scout tent with them. And he can't get out of a little plastic bag? Well, I ask you."

Dean stopped laughing long enough to say, "Maybe it was suicide."

"Right," she said with heavy sarcasm as she glanced at her watch. "I have to go to bed so I can get up and go to work tomorrow. Now I'll be up all night listening to every noise, every creak and groan this place makes. Why did you make me watch that stupid movie?"

"Me? You're the one who wanted to prove you could take it." He rose to his feet. "I suppose this is your cute way of telling me to vacate the premises. You want me to check under the bed for you?"

She gave him an indignant look. "I'm perfectly capable of looking under my own bed . . . and in the closet and the bathroom and on the window ledge and . . ."

He turned toward the bedroom. "I think we'll both feel better if I check."

"Dean . . . *Dean.*" She trailed after him. "This isn't necessary. I was just teasing. Dean, would you listen? I'm not worried."

In the process of opening the closet door, he paused and looked over his shoulder, one brow raised in skepticism.

"Okay," she said with a shrug, "I'm worried. While you're in there, look behind the overcoat at the back.

Then you can check for living dead in the bathroom.''

Giving a short bark of laughter, Dean walked into the bathroom and looked around. The area around the small sink was cluttered with cosmetics and other female paraphernalia. He picked up a vial of perfume, held it for a moment, then sat it back on the counter. A thick, white terry-cloth robe hung from a hook on the door. In white, Whitney looked like a sexy angel, and in his imagination, he could see her in the robe, the thick cloth emphasizing the slenderness of her body, her dark hair resting against the wide collar. Without thinking, he reached out to touch it, wondering if the smell of her flesh was still on—

"Hey," she called, "you're not being garroted or anything, are you?"

He jerked his hand back with an awkward movement. Stupid, stupid, *stupid.*

Reentering the bedroom, he found her sitting on the bed. "Nothing," he said, forcing a smile. "Not a body, bloody or otherwise."

"What is it in us that makes us want to be scared out of our wits?" she asked as he moved beyond her to check the window ledge, then make sure the window was locked.

"It's not just horror movies," she continued, pulling her feet up beneath her. "It's roller coasters and fast cars. Skydiving and jumping off bridges with rubber bands on our feet."

While she speculated on human nature, Dean watched her from the corners of his eyes, pretending not to, pretending that he was having trouble lowering the blinds.

He really wished she hadn't decided to sit on the bed. Because the image he had conjured up in the bathroom was nothing to the vision that took hold of him now. He saw himself pushing her back on the bed, her dark, silken hair spreading out across the pillow, her flesh bare and warm beneath his fingers.

With an abrupt movement, he shoved his hands into his pockets. Touching her, he thought sadly. Touching Whitney. It couldn't happen. Ever. Because if Dean got too close, she would be touched by more than his hands, more than his body. She would be touched by the past.

Whitney was bright and clear as crystal, and Dean wanted her to stay that way. She had only ever had brief glimpses of the darkness, and she didn't know that even now, years after the fact, the ugliness of his childhood still visited him. He had to keep that away from her. He would be damned if he would let the black imprint on his soul touch her.

Releasing a slow breath, he said, "All clear. I'll get out of your hair now."

At the front door, he pulled up a stiff smile. "Good night, sleep tight, don't let the psychotic killers bite." He opened the door, then paused. "I have to fly home tomorrow, but I should be back before you get home from work. If Lloyd is feeling better I'll take us all out to dinner. Eating your own cooking is making you lose weight."

"That's very funny. You're no wizard in the kitchen yourself."

He started through the door but again turned back to her. "You're not really going to be afraid tonight, are you?"

"I'm fine. I'm just *very sleepy,*" she said pointedly.

"Good...good." But instead of leaving, he leaned against the door frame and met her eyes. "Are you ready to talk about your mother yet?"

She bit her lip. "No— I don't know. Maybe."

Exhaling a little sigh, she leaned against the other side of the door, her face very close to his, and he could feel her soft breath on his lips.

"It's really weird, Dean," she said quietly. "Maybe pitiful is a better word. I'm so much in the habit of overlooking the things she does, always saying 'that's just Mother.'" She shook her head. "Sometimes something will remind me of her and I'll find myself smiling before I remember that I feel differently about her now. I don't want to be one of those people who expect everyone around them to be perfect, to never make mistakes, but— The thing is, if I found out she had an affair, or even that she had robbed a bank, I think I could come to grips with that. Because it wouldn't have been done to *me.* What she did, that was done to me, even though I know she doesn't see it that way. I keep telling myself that she really loves me, but sometimes I just don't know. How could she love me and hurt me like that?"

"She loves you," Dean said. "Even I don't doubt that. But she has different standards, different values than you and I do."

She caught her bottom lip between her teeth, and after a small pause, she shook her head again. "I just don't know what to think. I only know that I woke up one day and found that the woman I thought was my mother never existed. It's as though I made her up. Do I love her, or do I love my idea of her? If she's someone I don't know, how *could* I love her? You can't love a total stranger."

"Come on, Whit. You're looking at this from the wrong angle. There is one part of her that you didn't know. All the other parts were real. They just weren't the complete picture. You have to take the part you knew—the part you loved—and add this new part to it. You say you could allow her to make a mistake, and I believe you. You would have stood by her if she had run someone down in her Mercedes or something like that. But what she did wasn't a single act. And it wasn't just a careless mistake. She knew what she was doing. Which means there is a flaw in her personality, in her basic philosophy. And that's the part you're having trouble with. She really thought she was doing what was best. You know it was wrong and I know it was wrong, but faulty judgment is the flaw you have to allow in her."

She shook her head in a restless movement. "I don't know if I can."

"You don't have to do it tonight." He reached up and stroked her cheek with one finger. "I know you. You'll find some way to get through this."

If he moved his head a couple of inches he would be kissing her. Only a couple of inches.

Instantly he cursed himself for allowing the thought to form. Because now his mouth burned with the need to feel hers.

Straightening away from the door, he glanced at his watch. "This time I'm really leaving," he said, hearing stiffness in his own voice. "You get to bed and get some sleep."

When the door closed behind him, Dean stared at it for a long time. Leaving her was damned hard. And it got harder every time he had to do it.

Turning away, he walked the few steps to his apartment and unlocked the door. After he had turned on the light he stood for a moment and looked around the room. Furniture, magazines, plants. All the things necessary for human comfort were here and still the room felt barren. It was funny how two could equal full when just one less added up to empty.

Thirty minutes later Dean was lying in bed. He had left the window open because the air-conditioning was on the blink again, but there was almost no breeze. The room felt airless as he lay naked, his hands under his head, and stared at the ceiling.

There were times, like tonight, when he wondered if he was doing the right thing. Dear sweet heaven, did he even know what was right anymore?

Back when Whitney had been openly adoring, fighting his feelings for her had been damned hard. He hadn't thought it could get tougher than that. But he had been wrong. Dead wrong.

Even though he had always felt responsible for her, protecting her wasn't the only reason he had come back to Dallas. The plain fact was, Dean was here because he had no choice. Being without Whitney was like being without air. Like being without light. His life in San Antonio had stopped the minute she left, and a powerful need—the need to be with her, the need to see her smile and hear her laugh—had taken over his every thought.

His need for her had kept him awake at night, all kinds of wild thoughts visiting him. Whitney might be a hothouse flower, a Harcourt orchid, but she was an adult, free to make her own choices. Adults made love for a lot of reason, he told himself. They didn't have to be in love. Attraction, affection, even mutual need was enough for most people.

Dean had even managed, during those endless nights, to convince himself that making love to Whitney was his right. He had invested a lot of time and energy in her. It seemed only fair that he should be the first to touch her sweetness.

Dean knew she was a virgin. She had never been shy with him and would talk about anything that popped into her head. She had told him about her first kiss. She had told him about the fumbling in the dark that she hadn't taken seriously and had always stopped before it went too far.

And although she had never said the words aloud, Dean knew without a doubt that she had been waiting for him.

For *him*.

The idea twisted through him, leaving him drenched in perspiration. Whitney had waited for him. It was what she had wanted. Back then, before he had hurt her, she had wanted him to be her first and only love.

And during those long, frustrating nights back in San Antonio, Dean had told himself that no matter what happened between them in the future, no matter where their separate lives took them, it was right—it was *just*—that he should be her first lover. He had spent the better part of his life caring for Whitney. He deserved a return on his investment. If he were the first man to make love to her, he would be willing to call it even. Because then a part of her would always and forever belong to him.

In the dark of the night, when his body and soul ached for her, it had been easy for Dean to convince himself of a lot of foolish things. But the moment he had seen her again, he had known just how foolish the ideas had been.

Years of wanting Whitney and not having her should have dulled his sense of responsibility, but it hadn't worked out that way. Not where Whitney was concerned. He couldn't let her into his darkness. He couldn't stop being her protector, her hero.

And he was afraid that in the future, Whitney was going to need protecting. She was headed for trouble with her father.

When it happened, Dean was going to be there to hold her, the way he had always done in the past.

Chapter Ten

On the day of the company picnic, contrary to Whitney's predictions, it didn't rain. In fact, one couldn't have asked for a more beautiful day, and as it was a weekday, the employees of Tickner Toy Company had the small park pretty much to themselves.

The baseball game had begun soon after everyone arrived, and Whitney, wearing white shorts with a red blouse and red tennis shoes, was playing second base. Although she would most likely end up with skinned knees, she hadn't thought about diving for a ball when she had dressed for the picnic.

"Come on, Frankie!" she yelled. "You're doing great. Keep on striking them out."

After the first inning, Whitney's team was ahead by six runs, and since she still hadn't mastered the art of being a gracious winner, she was already a little hoarse from taunting the opposition.

When the two teams had chosen up sides, she and Lloyd somehow found themselves on opposing teams. Whitney had come to love her father all over again, the real Lloyd rather than her memory of him, but love and filial duty had nothing to do with baseball.

Whitney spotted Lloyd now, standing near the backstop, and waved to him. Cupping a hand to her mouth, she called, "You're going to get skunked, Lloyd!"

In response, Lloyd grinned in what she assumed was a show of false bravado. It wasn't long before she discovered her mistake.

After Frankie struck out a pretty redhead, Whitney squatted to retie her laces, and when she stood up again the next batter was in place.

For a moment she stared, her eyes narrowed, at the man who was swinging two bats over home plate, then she cut her eyes toward Lloyd and watched his smile widen. Lloyd had brought in a ringer. The next batter was Dean.

"That's illegal!" she yelled. "Throw the bum out. He doesn't work at the factory, and he's not a member of your family, Lloyd. Foul!"

"The rules don't say anything about family," Lloyd called back to her. "In fact, the rules don't say anything at all. We don't have any rules. Dean is my guest, and he's allowed to play on any team."

"He wasn't here when we chose up sides!" she protested. "You're trying to pull a fast one, Lloyd."

"Ralph twisted his ankle," someone else yelled. "Dean is a substitute. Are we supposed to play one man short?"

Dean glanced in her direction, one dark brow raised. "What's the matter, Mary?" he called. "Afraid of a little competition?"

Her response to that was to send him a very rude, very Italian gesture that set the spectators roaring with appreciative laughter.

Grumbling under her breath, she watched Dean choose his bat, then square up to the left side of home plate. Dean was good at sports. Very good.

"Don't try your fastball on him, Frankie," she yelled to the pitcher. "He may be a little slow mentally, but he can knock a fastball into next week."

Hearing her warning, the fielders began to back up. Since Dean was left-handed, Linelle, who was covering first, moved a couple of steps toward Whitney. Whitney changed her position as well, then leaned forward and settled her hands on her knees as she prepared to watch the action.

Frank checked the field—an unnecessary gesture since there were no runners on base—and, after winking at Whitney, wound up and threw his famous drop ball.

Apparently Dean had been watching Frankie earlier in the game and knew what was coming. Instead of swinging, he turned the bat at the last minute and in a seemingly casual movement, merely intersected the ball with a light tap, sending it skimming just over the ground toward right field.

"Bunt!" Whitney squealed. "You idiot, he bunted!"

After Linelle dove for the ball and missed it by inches, the outfielders began scrambling to reach it. And in the meantime, Dean had already passed first base.

Whitney moved back to her base and began jumping up and down, screaming for someone to throw the blasted ball. When a tall man finally scooped it up, Whitney lost track of Dean.

Raising her glove, she prepared to receive the ball. It was in the air coming toward her when Whitney heard people yelling, "Slide . . . *slide!*"

Dean took their advice. He reached second base a split second before the ball, sliding into Whitney and knocking her feet out from under her so that, after flailing wildly, she landed, full-length, on top of him.

Lloyd's team had finally gotten a man on base, and the spectators were going wild, hooting and stamping their feet in raucous celebration.

When Whitney felt one of Dean's hands clamped to her buttocks, she raised her head to look down at him.

"God, I love this game," he said, his eyes sparkling as he tightened his grip on her derriere.

Laughter caught her by surprise. Soon she was shaking with it, and she had to rest her forehead against his for a moment to catch her breath.

"Unhand my butt, you fool," she said as she pushed off him.

Rising to her feet, she offered him a hand. A show of sportsmanlike conduct never hurt anything. She could always get even with him later.

Dean's run set the tone for the rest of the game and an hour later it was all over but the crying. Lloyd's team had won by two runs.

She watched Dean mingling with her friends and co-workers, joking and laughing with them, and frowned. She knew Dean was in town because of his overdeveloped sense of responsibility, but that didn't explain why he was haunting her footsteps.

At times she saw something in him, a look, a tone of voice, that worried her. Some conflict, some inner struggle, was making him uneasy. And she was very much afraid the conflict was caused by his continuing absence from his law practice.

Dean was a dedicated attorney, and he had worked so hard to make his practice successful. Trying to maintain it from a distance would have to be frustrating for him.

She had gone out of her way to show him that she was capable of taking care of herself. He should have been convinced by now, but there was no mention of his returning to San Antonio. He was still there, as though he were waiting to rescue her from a disaster only he could foresee.

"What's worrying you?"

She glanced up to find Lloyd standing close beside her. "Dean . . . as usual," she said with a heavy sigh.

Lloyd shot a speculative glance toward where Dean was playing horseshoes with several others. "Looks to me like he's having a good time. What's the problem?''

"He shouldn't be here. I don't mean here at the picnic, I mean here in Dallas. He should be back in San Antonio in a courtroom. You've never seen him work, Lloyd, but he's some kind of boy wonder, the finest attorney seen in appellate court in years, they say." She pushed back her hair with a rough hand. "But he's so busy making sure I don't screw up my life, he's screwing up his own. I have to do something. I can't let him make stupid sacrifices for me. Not anymore."

"He's an adult," her father said with a shrug. "You can't tell him how to live his life any more than he can tell you how to live yours. You know what they say— a man's gotta do what a man's gotta do."

She gave a short laugh. "No, you're right. I can't tell him what to do, but I can show him that I'm getting a life going for myself. I can make him see that I don't need him to play big brother anymore."

Lloyd shoved his hands into his pockets and shook his head. "You've got your apartment, your job, new friends. From where I'm standing, that's a life. He's seen it. And he's still here."

She frowned. "I know, and I've been wondering about that. I've known Dean for a long time—for most of my life—and I never would have suspected him of being a male chauvinist, but I'm almost sure I know what his *hovering* is all about. He thinks I'm supposed to have a man to protect me. Not just a good friend like you, but my very own man. Stop laughing," she said, laughing with him as she punched him in the shoulder. "It's true. Why else would he still be here? He's waiting for me to go steady or something."

Still chuckling, he shook his head again. "I think you're wrong, but I'm not about to talk you out of the idea. I'm having too much fun watching you two. So now that you've spotted where the trouble is, what are you going to do about it?"

The question threw her for a moment. What *was* she going to do about it? She couldn't just sit around feeling guilty for ruining his life. Dean deserved better than that. It was her fault that he was in this mess, so she would just have to find a way to get him out of it.

She caught her bottom lip between her teeth as she concentrated on the problem, then after a moment, she raised her chin, shoved her thumbs through her belt loops, and glanced around the park. "I'm going to find me a man," she said, then walked away to the sound of Lloyd's laughter.

Whitney spent the next half hour scoping out the men at the picnic. By the time she was done she decided that finding an eligible man wasn't going to be as easy as she had thought. Several of the men she worked with had shown an interest in her, but Whitney knew she couldn't choose just any man. He had to be someone Dean would approve of. Someone Dean trusted.

The requirements weren't all that complicated, but as Whitney walked around the park, going from one group of people to the next, she made the unpleasant discovery that there were a lot of loose screws working at the toy factory.

Just when she was beginning to think it was hopeless, she caught sight of a stocky man in his midtwenties. She had forgotten all about Ralph Jenkins. Ralph was a sweet, shy man with blond hair and a pale complexion. His wasn't exactly a shining personality, and Whitney couldn't help wondering about a man in his late twenties who still lived with his mother, but Ralph was certainly someone Dean would find trustworthy.

"It's a good day for a picnic, isn't it?" Whitney said as she joined Ralph at a picnic table.

Eyeing her warily, the blond young man nodded and swallowed a couple of times in what seemed to be a nervous reaction to her presence.

Undaunted, Whitney leaned back against the concrete table and pressed on. "I think someone's getting people together for a volleyball game. Are you going to play?"

When he shook his head and swallowed yet again, Whitney shifted her position slightly. This was going to be tougher than she had thought. Ralph was watching her the way a man would watch a swaying cobra.

Gentling her lips into an encouraging smile, she said, "I'm sorry, Ralph. I forgot you twisted your ankle in the first inning of the game."

Again there was no verbal response. Whitney glanced around, frantically searching for a new subject. "Arnie brought his boat for anyone who wants to water-ski. What do you think? It should be fun. I know you won't be able to ski, but we could just ride around in the boat...and, you know, watch the others...or something."

Her last words dwindled away as Ralph began to swallow again and again in rapid succession. The scene took on surreal aspects and his somewhat prominent Adam's apple seemed to grow even more prominent, his neck more elongated.

She pursued the course of the maverick larynx with her eyes. Up...down. Then more rapidly—up and down, up and down...

And then Ralph spoke. "I don't—"

She leaned forward hopefully, but instead of finishing the thought, he broke off and swallowed—again.

Whitney cleared her throat to suppress a hysterical giggle. "Is it your ankle? Is it still painful?" She had given up hoping for a real conversation, but was perfectly willing to carry on alone. "Say, I have an idea. Why don't we sit under a tree while they're cooking the hamburgers? When they're done I can fetch yours for you. That way you can stay off that bum ankle, and you and I will have a chance to get to know more about each—"

"Ralph, your mother is looking for you. She's entered the three-legged race and needs a cheering section."

She swung around and found Dean on the other side of the picnic table, his knee bent as he rested one leg on the bench.

Turning back to Ralph, Whitney saw an expression of relief cross his thin face before he stood and limped away.

"Why did you do that?" she asked, rising to her feet in exasperation. "Ralph and I were having an interesting conversation."

Dean raised one brow. "I beg your pardon, did you say conversation? I guess I don't understand all the finer nuances of the word. Does conversation mean that one person talks while the other sweats and shakes?"

She raised her chin belligerently. "You don't know anything about it. Ralph was just beginning to loosen up."

He gave a loud bark of laughter. "Sure he was. If he got any looser, he would have passed out. The poor man was scared to death. Face it, Whit, when you turn on the sizzle, you separate the men from the boys. Ralph is a nice guy, but he's definitely not up to your speed."

Her eyes widened in indignant surprise. "I don't know what you're talking about. You act like I'm some kind of femme fatale. I don't exactly have a long trail of broken hearts behind me. You know better than anyone that I'm as virginal as they come. Untouched by human hands. Ninety-nine and forty-four one-hundredths percent pure."

There was a barely discernible pause, then Dean slowly ran his gaze over her in what seemed like a deliberate examination of her body. "I know things about you that even you don't know," he said finally, his voice low.

Whitney stared in shock, taken aback by the unconscious sensuality that flared in his dark eyes.

At least, she thought it was unconscious. Of course it was unconscious, she admonished silently. Dean had never turned a seductive look in her direction, and she had a feeling she probably should be grateful for that fact. Because, judging by her reaction to a look she had mistaken for lust, she was pretty sure she wouldn't be able to handle the real thing.

Then, in the next moment, as if he had flipped an invisible switch, Dean was back to normal.

"You're forgetting Ralph's mother. Have you met Mrs. Jenkins?" he asked with a wicked grin. "Ralph might be tempted to jump into the volcano, but you can be sure his mama would drag him back by the ear before he could even get to the edge." He reached across the table and tweaked her nose. "I think maybe you'd better pick on someone your own size."

"Oh, go eat a bug," she grumbled.

As she walked away, she heard his laughter and realized she was not only providing entertainment for Lloyd but for Dean, as well.

Let them laugh, she told herself. She knew what she had to do and she was going to do it. If she had to interview every unmarried man at the toy factory, if she had to resort to checking out the men at the paper factory, she would find someone to start dating on a regular basis.

It was while she was talking to Louise Grendt, an older woman who worked in shipping, about her eligible nephew—the time Roy Gene had spent in federal prison was nothing more than an unfortunate mistake, the woman assured her—that Whitney happened to notice Frankie Halloran.

He was standing at a barbecue grill tending hamburgers, and when he spotted her, he turned to wave, yelling something she couldn't decipher due to the fact that his mouth was full of potato chips.

Whitney had finished her conversation with Louise and had taken several steps away when she stopped in her tracks and swung around.

Frankie, she thought, staring at the group around the barbecue grill. *Frankie.*

Whitney spent the next few minutes tracking down Linelle. She eventually found the blonde washing her hands at a water fountain.

"Linelle," Whitney said, grasping the woman's arm. "Linelle, listen, can I borrow Frankie? No, wait, let me start again."

Whitney splashed some water on her face, then drew in a slow breath as she pulled her thoughts together. "How's it going with you and Frankie?" she asked with a polite smile. "Are you making any progress?"

"Some," Linelle admitted, her eyes suspicious. "What are you up to?"

"Nothing...at least nothing that should make you nervous. It's just that I need to date Frankie a couple of times. Wait, don't hit me. I'll explain everything later. And, it's not what you're thinking. If I were interested in him, would I be here asking your permission? No, of course I wouldn't. I'd be with Frankie, making my move. I just didn't want you to get mad at me if you hear that I've gone out with him, because it won't be like a real date. In fact, I'll probably spend the whole time talking about you...and I promise I won't let him take me anywhere in his handy little Den of Sin.'' Every inch of the inside of Frankie's van was covered with plush red carpet and black satin cushions. ''So what do you say? Can I have him for a little while?''

Linelle looked confused. ''Why are you asking me? Do I look like his mother? Frankie's a grown man. He makes up his own mind about who he—''

''Linelle,'' Whitney said, her voice pleading.

''Okay, okay.'' The blonde wiped her damp hands on her shorts. ''But only for a couple of dates. And I find out he's taken you anywhere near our parking place, you'll be trying to find out which floor wax works best on a bald head. Do you hear me, Mary?'' Linelle called this last out as, with a triumphant whoop, Whitney turned and hurried away.

Whitney didn't know why she hadn't thought of Frankie before. He was perfect. Dean seemed to like him, and he certainly couldn't say that Frankie Halloran wasn't up to her speed. Frankie could pass a roadrunner like it was standing still.

''Frankie!'' she called, waving when he glanced over his shoulder.

When Whitney reached him, he put down his spatula and struck a bodybuilder pose. "I knew you couldn't resist me for long," he said. "What was it that got to you? The sight of my manly chest?" He clenched his fists, flexing his pectoral muscles. "My outstanding athletic ability?"

"It's the way you cook hamburgers," she said, smiling as she glanced beyond him to the rising smoke. "I do admire a slipshod man."

The next few minutes were spent in casual flirtation—no one could flirt better than Frankie—but when Whitney spotted Dean making his way toward them, she decided the subtle approach was taking too long.

Grabbing Frankie's arm, she said, "Quick, can you come to my place for dinner this Friday?"

"Ah, she's getting desperate," Frankie said, closing his eyes and inhaling with pleasure. "What time?"

"Eight." She glanced over her shoulder again. Dean was getting closer. His eyes were narrowed, his jaw clenched, in a way she remembered of old.

"You got yourself a date," Frankie told her. "I'll be there with a bottle of wine, a bouquet of posies and the gorgeous bod."

"Great . . . terrific." The words were said over her shoulder as she hurried away from the barbecue pit, but she hadn't taken more than a few steps when Dean grabbed her arm and swung her around to face him.

"What devious little plots are you concocting this time, Whitney?"

"Shush," she hissed, looking around nervously. "I'm Mary, remember?"

"I don't care if you're Maynard G. Krebs. I want to know what you're up to?"

"I'm not doing anything except what you've always wanted me to do," she told him as they moved farther away from the group around the barbecue grill.

Hearing the defensive note in her voice, she shook her head impatiently. "You told me to get a life," she told him in an emphatic whisper. "You told me to get my own life. You told me to be a person. This is what people do. They mix and mingle with members of the opposite sex." She looked at him, studying his face as they walked. "You like Frankie. You know you do. And what do you want to bet he can handle my so-called sizzle?"

Dean frowned down at her. Frankie might be able to handle it, but the fact didn't give Dean any comfort. In fact it made him nervous as hell.

Whitney was right, of course. This is what he had said, often and loudly, that he wanted for her. But what he said and what he felt in his gut were worlds apart.

Dean spent the next few days driving himself crazy, thinking about the prospect of Whitney being with someone else, laughing with someone else, kissing someone else, touching someone else. Since he had come to Dallas, Dean had spent the better part of each day on the phone—with clients or his secretary or Sam—and although it wasn't a perfect situation, in general it had worked out pretty well. But that was when he could keep his mind on what he was doing. During the days after the picnic, things began to go downhill in a hurry. Unable to concentrate on anything but Whitney, Dean found himself snapping at everyone he talked to. By Thursday, Sam had told him to drop dead and his secretary was threatening to resign.

Whitney hadn't mentioned her date with Frankie—in fact she had done her best to avoid Dean all week—but Lloyd had informed him that Frankie would be at her apartment at eight. Which was why, by eight o'clock on Friday night, Dean was in a murderous mood. He couldn't watch television, and he wasn't interested in food.

After pacing around his small living room for half an hour, he left his apartment and went to Rick's.

"I've never seen anyone like her," Dean told Lloyd.

The two men were sitting at the bar at Rick's as Dean finished another Little Mary story.

"If she had simply kept her mouth shut, she wouldn't have gotten into nearly as much trouble," he explained with a reminiscent smile. "But try telling her that. If she has something to say, she's damn well going to say it."

"She probably counted on the fact that you would bail her out," Lloyd said.

"I always did what I could," Dean admitted. "And she thought I could do anything. She didn't understand that a boy from the wrong side of the tracks doesn't have a whole lot of pull with school officials. Or with cautious parents. But at least when I couldn't fix it, I was there to help her get it out of her system.''

He shook his head slowly. ''She's not like other people. And it's not just her looks or her willingness to fight for what she believes in. There's something unique, something singular, about her spirit.''

He paused, staring into the mirror behind the bar, then after a moment he shook his head and stared into his beer glass. ''She's strong and wise, vulnerable and funny. And you wouldn't believe how perceptive she is, Lloyd. You never have to wonder if she understands something or not. She can grasp an idea before it's even fully formed in your mind.'' He laughed. ''Of course, she's also the most intractable, pigheaded female it's ever been my misfortune to meet. When she gets an idea in her head, you couldn't pry it loose with a crowbar. She just won't let go.''

''And you can't let her go,'' Lloyd said quietly. It wasn't a question. It was a flat statement of fact.

''I'm trying, Lloyd,'' he said, drawing in a slow breath. ''God knows, I'm trying.''

After glancing at his watch, Dean downed the last of his beer and slid off the stool.

He went back to his apartment and paced the floor for a while, checking his watch every few seconds. It was after eleven. Surely by now Frankie had gone home.

Dean stopped pacing. If he hadn't gone home, maybe it was time someone gave him a shove in the right direction.

Slamming the door behind him, Dean walked the few steps to her apartment and knocked on her door. He waited a couple of seconds, then pounded on it.

The door swung open and Whitney stood there, staring at him. She wore jeans and a clingy blue silk blouse that made her eyes even brighter.

When she didn't speak, Dean looked beyond her and saw her date sitting on the floor. Spread out on the coffee table was a board game.

Dean returned his gaze to Whitney. "I need to borrow a cup of sugar," he said, his voice flat.

She raised one slender brow. "Baking again?" she asked sweetly before standing aside so he could come into the apartment.

"You bake, Dean?" Frankie asked. His voice was only casually interested, as though he were perfectly willing to believe that Dean spent all his free time kneading bread dough and whipping up batches of cookies.

"Just don't think about entering the Pillsbury bake-off this year," Dean told the other man, then glanced at the coffee table. "Trivial Pursuit? Watch out for her, Frankie. She cheats."

"You lie," Whitney said, her blue eyes reflecting a mixture of indignation and amusement.

Dean made himself comfortable on the couch, letting Frankie know he wasn't leaving any time soon.

After a moment, Frankie glanced at his watch. "Gee, look at the time." He stood up and stretched noisily. "Guess I'd better be going."

After casting a vengeful look in Dean's direction, Whitney walked her date to the door, and Frankie, confident of his charms, didn't bother to lower his voice as he asked her if she would go to a movie with him.

"I'd like that," Whitney said. "Catch me on break Monday and we can talk about it...in *private.*"

She closed the door behind him and walked slowly back to the couch, then stood in front of Dean with her hands on her hips. "Now do you want to tell me what that was all about? You knew I had company. And don't give me that garbage about needing sugar. You bought a bag last Wednesday."

He leaned his head back and stared at the ceiling.

Dean's expression, his *mood,* puzzled Whitney. "What's going on, Dean? I know you want me to make a new life for myself. I guess, somewhere in the back of my mind, I've always known it. But after that little slash-and-burn psychology session in your bedroom— Well, I may be a little dense, but I think I got the point. So that's what I'm trying to do now. Make a new life for myself. I thought Frankie would be a good place to start. Nothing serious, just a little foray into the wonderful world of adult relationships. Dipping my toes into sexual waters, as it were."

He turned his head toward her, his dark eyes blazing. "You're not ready to dip anything anywhere yet," he said in a clipped voice. "You're too inexperienced."

She snorted her skepticism. "At the picnic you were full of talk about sizzle and volcanoes. Now suddenly I'm too inexperienced?"

"Sizzle is a quality," he said tightly. "It isn't practical experience."

She threw up her hands in exasperation. "You beat everything, you know that? How am I supposed to get experience if you keep bird-dogging me? This isn't exactly a spectator sport we're talking about here."

He was staring at the ceiling again, his expression closed. Whitney didn't know what he was thinking, and that fact made her extremely nervous.

"Who taught you how to play baseball?" he asked, his voice abrupt.

"You did."

"Who taught you how to ride a bicycle? To drive a car? To throw a dirty punch in a fight?"

"We both know you taught me all those things. So what's your point?" she asked in frustration.

Dean turned his head slowly to meet her eyes. She stared at him in irritated confusion until suddenly the truth broke through and left her gasping for breath.

Chapter Eleven

Blood rushed to Whitney's face, and the room grew uncomfortably hot as Dean continued to stare at her.

"You're not suggesting— You *are,* aren't you?" She swung away from him, smoothing her hands across her heated cheeks. "You've lost your mind. You've finally and completely lost your mind."

After a moment she glanced cautiously over her shoulder. He was watching her closely still, as though gauging her reaction.

Keeping her eyes on his face, she moved to sit beside him on the couch. "Are you sure you feel all right?" she asked, frowning in concern.

He laughed silently. "You sound like you're thinking about taking my temperature. I'm not crazy and I'm not feverish."

"Then what in hell is going on?" She was genuinely confused. "You were practically begging me to cut those old ties that strangle. You said—"

"The ties never strangled," he interrupted, his voice quiet and emphatic. "Never. I thought it would be best—for *you*—if you stepped back a little. I thought you should put some space between yourself and a relationship that began when you were too young to know better. I simply wanted you to look at your feelings from an objective distance."

After a moment she said, "You seemed to have done a lot of planning for me. And you made an awful lot of decisions without asking about my druthers. But maybe it's unfair of me to resent that. I certainly didn't give you any reason to believe I could make those decisions on my own."

She paused, chewing on her lower lip. "But now you've obviously changed your mind and come up with a whole new plan for me," she said slowly. "Because— I may be way off base here, but it seems to me that what you're suggesting is not going to put any distance between me and anything."

He reached out and cupped her neck with warm fingers. His eyes were half-closed so that she couldn't see his expression. "I haven't changed my mind, Whit. I still want you to make objective decisions. When it's time," he added firmly. "When you're ready to handle whatever comes along."

She pulled away from the hand that was destroying her ability to think. "And sex comes under the heading of Whatever Comes Along? Couldn't you just buy me one of those Now-That-You're-a-Woman books that mothers give to their teenage daughters?"

"Does the idea of making love with me embarrass you?" he asked, his voice blunt.

"I—" She broke off and shook her head in a helpless movement.

He glanced away from her. "That day you walked into my bedroom, just before you left San Antonio, you wanted me that day."

Whitney's breath caught in her throat, and she closed her eyes in self-defense. "The gloves are off now," she said wryly, her voice weak.

Saying she wanted him was like saying a roaring furnace was a little blaze. She had never felt anything as powerful, before or since.

"I wanted you, too, Whitney."

The quiet words dropped like a bombshell between them. Opening her eyes, she studied his face and knew he was telling her the truth.

She ran her tongue over the inner edge of her lower lip in a nervous gesture. "But you— Why did you hide it? Why did you say all those things?"

He frowned. "You were brought up by people who didn't know anything about real life. I guess I just got used to protecting you. And I was afraid you would get sidetracked. I pulled out the...the 'slash-and-burn psychology,' as you called it—" he didn't relish using her vivid description ''—because I didn't want you to think an affair with me was the real thing.''

Whitney let the explanation sink in. Dean was saying he wanted her. But he was also saying he didn't love her. She knew that. She had known it when she left San Antonio. Hearing the words shouldn't have caused the suffocating pain in her chest. Hearing an acknowledged truth shouldn't hurt quite so much.

Moistening her lips, she drew in a slow breath to steady her voice. ''And now?''

He shrugged. ''Whether you're a Harcourt, a Grant, or Mary White, you're an adult. Old enough to make your own decisions, old enough to handle a physical attraction.''

''Oh, yeah?'' Her tone was openly skeptical.

''Yeah,'' he said with a slight smile. ''But I don't want this to be something that we simply slide into. No being carried away by the heat of the moment. I couldn't handle the thought of you waking up tomorrow regretting what happened tonight. We both have to know what we're getting into before we make another move.''

''Are we going to sign a contract?'' Without waiting for a response she rose abruptly to her feet. ''No, you stay here,'' she said when he started to get up. ''I need some time alone…to think. I'll go make us some coffee,'' she added on her way out of the room.

Dean watched her leave. What in hell was he doing? She was right, he had finally lost his mind. This wasn't what he had intended when he came here tonight. He was simply going to make sure that Frankie wasn't pulling any fast moves on her.

A short, contemptuous laugh escaped him. Frankie wasn't the problem. The only one trying to pull a fast move around here was Dean himself.

He stood up and was almost to the kitchen to tell her to forget the whole thing, that it had been a bad joke, when he stopped, shoved a hand though his hair and walked back to the couch.

Whitney said that Dean had been making decisions for her without her knowledge or consent, and to a certain extent she was right about that. If he really believed Whitney was a mature, capable adult, then he had to allow her to make this decision on her own. It wasn't his place to tell her to forget it. Only Whitney knew what was best for her.

He had put his proposition to her in an unconventional way, but even if he had said, "How's about it, kid?" it would lead to the same thing. She would make a decision—of her own free will, and based on her own needs and desires—whether to accept or reject his offer.

And if she decided—on her own—that she was better off rejecting it, then the fact that Dean wanted her more than life itself was something he would have to deal with . . . on his own.

In the kitchen, Whitney put the coffee on, then stood and watched as it slowly ran into the pot. Could she handle it? Could she come away from an affair with Dean without permanent injury? Could she accept the fact that when he touched her, he was touching only the outside, making no effort to reach what was inside her?

The pot had been full of coffee for a good quarter of an hour before Whitney finally decided that it didn't matter if she could handle an affair with Dean or not. She would almost certainly get hurt, but that had never stopped her before. Whitney didn't believe in foregoing the wonderful things in life just because some bad might come along with them. If this was all she would ever have of Dean, it was more than she had had yesterday.

She walked back into the living room, carrying two cups of coffee. She handed one to him and sat down, cradling the other cup between her fingers.

Several minutes of silence passed. Dean was taking a sip of coffee when she finally said, "Okay, let's do it."

He choked. "Damn it, Whitney, you made me burn my mouth."

"Want me to kiss it and make it better?"

He drew in a sharp breath and turned his head slowly toward her. "Yes...yes, I want that very much."

Turning slightly in her seat, she leaned toward him. This was what she wanted. It was what she had always wanted. But now that it was finally going to happen, she felt awkward. She had always imagined their first real kiss would come about in a more natural, less calculated way.

She drew back a little and wiped her mouth with the back of her hand, then glancing at him, said, "I'm getting there. Don't rush me." She pushed the hair from her forehead. "I can do this." She leaned forward and almost immediately pulled back again. "But on the other hand, there's something to be said for being carried away by the heat of the moment. I feel like there's a script for this and I've forgotten all my lines."

He gave a soft laugh and framed her face with his hands. "Want me to help?"

Pulling away from his hands, she rose abruptly to her feet. "I don't know what's wrong with me. It's not like I've never been kissed, for pity's sake. I even did a little petting when I first got into college, back when I—"

"I remember." His voice was rough. "You told me all about it, every damned time it happened."

"There weren't that many times."

"There were enough. I had to sit and listen to you tell me about some snot-nosed kid touching you."

She stared at him in silence. Something about his tone, something about the look in his dark eyes, nagged at her.

"I don't remember any of them being snot-nosed," she said, her voice distracted as she tried to analyze the information that was being received by her brain. "In fact, I'm almost sure they weren't. I happen to be very discriminating."

She continued to stare at him, a frown creasing her brow. "You sound mad. Did it really bother you to know that I was ... getting close to other men?"

"Bother me?" He gave a short, harsh laugh. "That doesn't even begin to cover it. I told myself that I was simply being protective. That I didn't want you getting into something you couldn't handle. But that didn't explain why I had the urge to pound some heads on the pavement."

She gave a soft whistle. So that was it.

"Ain't life strange," she muttered, then walking to the window, she pushed the curtain aside to look out.

The minor sexual skirmishes he was referring to had taken place during her first year at college. Six years ago. He had wanted her for six years?

Her first reaction to his amazing disclosure was relief that on those long, lonely nights when all she had had of him were dreams, Dean was feeling something similar. But relief was soon superceded by anger. All those lonely nights. If he had told her this years ago, those long, lonely nights wouldn't have happened.

Then finally she began to think about the implications of Dean's revelation. He said he wanted her. He wanted an affair with her. Period. And he was careful to tell her that she wasn't to make more out of it than there was. Nothing but good old-fashioned lust.

He was fooling himself. She didn't know why, but he was fooling himself. Lust was notoriously fickle. It wasn't the kind of thing that hung around for six years.

As she stared into the darkness, the hand that was holding the curtain to the side began to shake. She wanted to tell him. She wanted to share this as she shared everything else with him. She wanted to turn around and say, "You fool, you're in love with me." She wanted to list all the facts and show him why her conclusion was undeniable.

Whitney had to clamp her teeth together to keep from confronting him with the truth. She couldn't do it. She couldn't tell him. Not yet. Dean was the most intelligent man she knew. He understood all about people and motivations. And he spent a lot of time examining his own actions and reactions. Which meant that something was keeping him from this particular truth. For some reason, he was hiding from his feelings for her. Dean didn't want to be in love with her.

There was only a little pain attached to the realization. It would have been better if he were able to return her love freely and joyfully, but she had long ago accepted the fact that he was complicated, mentally and emotionally. This was the man she had loved all her life. He was worth fighting for. He was worth waiting for.

"What are you thinking about?" he asked now.

When she turned around, she found him close behind her, a frown worrying his features.

She raised one hand to smooth away the lines from his face. "I'm thinking that I'm through thinking. I'm thinking that thinking uses up time that could be spent—" she wiggled her eyebrows "—more productively." She moved closer. "Did you notice how I wiggled my eyebrows? That's to let you know I was making an oblique sexual reference. Now this—" she stood on her tiptoes and brushed her lips across his, smiling when she heard his sharply indrawn breath "—there is nothing at all oblique about this. This is—"

The rest of her explanation was cut off as he wrapped his arms around her and pulled her tightly to him. He molded her body to his, touching her with hands that shook, as though he had been waiting for a long time to feel this particular feeling and couldn't wait a second longer.

His breathing was labored when he pulled back a little and rested his forehead against hers. "You remembered your lines," he said in a hoarse whisper.

Her laugh was cut off by his mouth. The taste of him, the feel of him, had filled Whitney's dreams, waking and sleeping, for most of her life, and now it was no fantasy. It was real. His kiss set off an explosion of sensations and she couldn't get enough of it. Afraid he would change his mind, she clasped his neck and frantically sought his tongue with her own, pushing her body even closer to his.

Now that she knew he loved her, she was fearless, and she felt the shock of her response rock through him. A deep groan came from deep in his chest, and he bent slightly, picking her up in his arms without interrupting the fiery kiss.

He carried her into her bedroom and fell with her onto the bed. Then he was touching her and it was better than all her dreams put together. All the long, lonely nights were forgotten as they hungrily explored territory that had been forbidden them only hours ago, staking claim with their lips and tongues and fingers.

Even in the heat of passion, Dean was still protective. He didn't rush her. He made sure she was ready before he took the next step. He discarded his shirt, but merely unbuttoned her silk blouse, easing her into total intimacy. He had to take it slow. He had to make this right for her.

But Whitney didn't want cautious moves. She had been waiting for him, starving for him, for most of her life, until now the aching need had taken over completely. She didn't wait for him to remove her clothes. She was out of them, tossing them away without a thought.

When Dean pulled away from her to take off the rest of his clothes, he stood for a moment beside the bed staring at her in awe. The pale body, the midnight hair fanning out on the white pillow, made him catch his breath as her beauty went right to the heart of him.

He had finally allowed his true feelings to surface and the power of them knocked him sideways. How could he have lived so long without this? How could he have managed without knowing what it was like to touch her, to feel her hands on him?

His whole body was shaking as he joined her on the bed, and he whispered incomprehensible words of love in her ear as he lifted her and made them one.

For Whitney, there was no room for fear, no room for pain. As she had always known, their bodies were specifically made for the purpose of loving each other. But she hadn't known that this moment would bring sensations, wilder and more incredibly beautiful than anything that had gone before. How could she know that each movement, each heated caress, would be more deeply felt than the one that went before?

As they moved together, the moonlight streamed across the bed, illuminating naked flesh against naked flesh, hunger matching hunger. And then, together, they let the feelings gather strength. Building and growing until there was nothing in the wide world other than the sweet, fierce sensations. It was around them and in them. It was in their heads and their bodies and their hearts. It bound them forever and finally gave them peace.

Dean felt the impact of the fury through a dense, black fog, then gradually the fog dissolved and he saw the two people. His stepfather stood before him, a raging giant, towering over everything in the room, one tightly clenched fist raised, his features twisted in violent anger. Dean's mother looked tiny in comparison as she cowered in an armchair with torn upholstery. She was crying. Helplessly. Hopelessly. Fear shook through every inch of her fragile body.

In the next moment Dean was no longer viewing the scene, he was living it. He was inside the man he hated most in the world. And in the torn armchair, Whitney shook and cried. Then he knew he wasn't looking at her through his stepfather's eyes. It was his own eyes. His own body. Dean was the despised, raging giant. And he was making Whitney cry. He was hurting her. His dear, sweet Whitney. He was making her tremble with fear.

Please God, he couldn't let it happen. He had to get away from her. He had to run. Run!

He struggled to turn his sluggish giant's body away from her, but finally he was at the door, forcing it open.

Dear sweet heaven, she was there beside him! Holding onto him, pulling him back, trying to make him stay. He opened his mouth, but no words came out. No words to tell her, to make her understand that he had to protect her. He had to keep her safe.

Groans born of frustration and fear burned in his throat, but still there was no sound, and the look in her eyes was killing him, ripping him up inside.

Whitney...for pity's sake, Whitney! Please, please—

Whitney turned her head slowly on the pillow and watched Dean sleep. Early morning sunlight had been floating through the curtains for almost an hour, but she didn't want to wake him. She wanted to savor the pleasure of seeing his head on the pillow next to her. It was a little bit of intimacy that was as unexpected as it was thrilling.

Whitney was convinced she hadn't made a mistake last night. Dean loved her. She was sure of it. But something was keeping him from acknowledging that fact, even to himself. Maybe he was afraid of commitment. His mother had gone through two bad marriages, two divorces. It would be no wonder if he was afraid the same thing would happen to him.

She would simply have to show him that he didn't have to be afraid of love. She would wear him down until eventually he had no choice but to marry her and be happy for the rest of his life. Because she could make him happy. She knew she could. She would be a good wife to him. She would give him so much love and happiness, he wouldn't know what hit him. She would make him forget all about the past.

When he muttered in his sleep and moved restlessly, she couldn't stand not touching him for one second. Brushing a kiss across the top of his ear, she said, "You're awake now, aren't you, Dean? I wouldn't be taking advantage of a helpless man if I happened to touch you here—" she moved her hand down his body "—would I?"

His eyes opened abruptly, and for a moment he held himself stiffly, then he released his breath in a sigh and grabbed her, flipping over to pin her with his body.

"If you did that, I might have to retaliate and touch you here." He smoothed one hand across her breast, letting his thumb linger on the nipple. "Or here... or—"

He broke off and groaned when they heard a knock at the front door. Rolling off her, he folded his arms behind his head and sighed deeply. A martyr's sigh.

"Don't forget where you were," she said as she climbed out of bed and pulled on a short robe. "I'll gun down the idiot at the door, then be right back."

Before she left the room, she had to bend over him for one last kiss. Two. Three.

She kissed his cheek. "You have the sexiest cheek-bones in creation." And his forehead. "The brow of a genius, honest to God." And his chin. "Stub-born...too stubborn for your own good." And his mouth. "I don't think I can leave these lips. I really don't."

Shaking with laughter, he pulled her down on top of him. He was giving her a sample of his irresistible lips when they heard the knock again.

Dean stood up with her in his arms, then set her on her feet. "Get rid of them," he ordered as he ran a hand over her buttocks. "Get rid of them fast."

On her way to the front door, she straightened her robe and pushed her fingers through her hair. If a salesman was at her front door, he would be on the receiving end of the fastest turndown in history.

But it wasn't a salesman. It was her father.

"Lloyd," she said in surprise as she tried to gather her thoughts. "I thought you had some kind of in-ventory thing you were supposed to take care of to-day."

"It was canceled. I just wanted to—" Looking be-yond her, he broke off and smiled. "Good morning, Dean."

Whitney glanced around and saw Dean standing in the doorway to the bedroom. Although he had pulled on his jeans, even the slowest observer would have known that he had just gotten out of bed. And Whit-ney's father was definitely not slow.

"Lloyd," Dean said politely.

Her father was still smiling. "I'll come back later," he said, turning away.

Whitney grabbed his arm and pulled him into the apartment. "No you won't. You're going to stay and have breakfast with us. Dean was just saying how hungry he is. Weren't you saying that, Dean?"

"My very words." He walked farther into the living room. "Join us for breakfast, Lloyd. I promise I won't let her anywhere near a skillet."

She made a small huffing noise. "Are you implying— I'll have you know I scramble a mean egg."

"Mean is right. When she gets through with them, those suckers are tough enough to fight back," Dean said as he pushed open the door to the kitchen. "Stop sulking, Mary. If you behave yourself, we'll let you make the toast.

A short while later Whitney was sitting on the kitchen counter as she scraped the black parts off the last piece of toast.

"Is it my fault the stupid toaster is defective? You helped me pick it out, Lloyd." She put the toast on the plate with the rest and hopped down. "Besides, I've heard that carbon is good for the digestion."

Both men made rude noises, but they ate the toast anyway. And Whitney had to admit that Dean made a good breakfast. Maybe he would teach her.

Having breakfast with the two men she loved was destined to become one of those bright spots in life that one looks back on with an automatic smile: Dean and Lloyd arguing about baseball and jazz; Dean and

Whitney fighting over the last of the strawberry jam; Lloyd popping Whitney's hand with his fork when she tried to take more than her share of the bacon.

When it was over—Lloyd insisted on staying to help with the dishes—Whitney hated to see her father leave. She knew he was trying to give them their privacy, and she wanted to tell him that he wasn't intruding. He was her father and therefore a part of their life. But she didn't say anything.

When the front door closed behind him, Whitney turned to Dean. "I've got to do it. I've got to tell him. He likes me now. Don't you think he likes me now? Don't you think we're real, true friends?"

"He loves you, Whit," Dean said quietly. "And you need to tell him soon. Because the longer you put if off, the harder it's going to be on both of you."

"You're right. You're right. I know you're right. But I need to work out how I'm going to do it. I need to figure out exactly what I'm going to say to him."

He put his arms around her and pulled her close. "Be prepared for some anger, honey. I don't want to scare you, but you need to remember how you reacted when you discovered your mother's deception."

She nodded against his chest, then drew in a slow breath. "I called her a couple of days ago."

"Did you? I'm proud of you."

"Don't be too proud," she said, her voice rueful. "I was barely civil." She gave a short laugh. "Not that Mother noticed. It was like I was away at college or something. She told me everything that was going on in San Antonio. How they missed me at the hospital benefit, things like that. She never once mentioned Daddy. I knew it would be this way. I knew she would pretend it had never happened.''

He stroked her hair. ''Everyone has his own way of coping. She wouldn't know it was hurting you.''

''Do you really think it would make a difference? I mean, if the impossible happened and she actually wondered if her actions would hurt me, would it make a difference to her?''

She pulled out of his arms and walked a couple of steps away from him. ''Would you listen to me? When did I turn into a whiner?'' She reached out and punched his arm. ''And why on earth did you let me?''

It had just occurred to her that Dean had never once complained about his mother's neglect or his stepfather's abuse. Compared to what his parents had put him through, Whitney had led a fairy-tale life, and she was suddenly very much ashamed of herself.

''You weren't whining,'' he told her. ''You have a perfect right to be angry. And talking about it is one way of working out that anger.''

But not Dean's way, she told herself silently. His life was filled with injustices. Injustices that he carried alone.

Whitney would change that. If she had to pry the words out of him with a tire iron, she would make him share all his pain and anger with her. She would make him see that it was all right to give a little bit of it to her.

They spent the rest of the day doing silly things—her idea. Now that she was free to love him, she wanted to give him back some of his missing childhood. She made him take her to Six Flags Over Texas, where they ate pink things on a stick and curly fries. They rode the giant wooden roller coaster and the Cliffhanger and the Runaway Mine Train. They played every game of chance in the arcade and came home tired and hot and happy, with their arms full of cheap stuffed animals.

Dean spent the night with her again, but something about his mood puzzled Whitney. She couldn't figure out what was going on in his mind. He still wanted her—most of the time he could barely keep his hands off her—but there were too many brooding silences between them. It was almost as though he regretted their new relationship.

In the days that followed, Dean's strange mood continued. Each time they made love he seemed to be fighting a silent battle. And each time, when he finally took her to bed, his reaction was explosive and reckless, as though he were throwing good sense to the wind. As though he fought his feelings until they grew too powerful to control.

Dean had always been big on control. And maybe that was the problem. Maybe he resented the fact that his feelings for her were so strong, stronger even than his control.

On Thursday, almost a week after they first made love, Whitney was having lunch in the cafeteria at the factory when she decided she would have to force the issue. Even if she got hurt, she had to get him to talk about what was going on inside him.

After work, as soon as she had taken a shower and changed her clothes, she went straight to his apartment.

"Did you have a good day?" she asked when he let her in. "Is the Sanderson case going all right?"

"Average to the first question and the way I expected to the second," he said dryly as he moved to sit on the couch.

"That's good...that's good." She shoved her hands into the pockets of her shorts. "Dean... Dean, I've been doing some thinking."

He raised one dark brow. "Now there's a scary thought."

"You're so funny." She moved to sit on the coffee table in front of him. "You told me that I was too inexperienced. Well, that's changed. I've had lots of experience. Wonderful, exciting experience."

His features were tight as he studied her face. "Get to the point, Whitney."

"Well, if the object was to clue me in on sex, I'm clued. You have to admit I wasn't slow in picking it up."

Whitney stared beyond him, avoiding his eyes. She knew she was taking a big chance, but some things were worth taking a chance on. Dean was worth taking a chance on.

"I'm probably ready for a solo flight," she continued. "Well, not solo really, but I think I'm ready to go up without my esteemed instructor. Don't you think so? I mean, now that you know I can *do* it, you don't have to worry about me anymore. You could probably even move back to San Antonio now and get your practice back in shape.''

"You've met someone new?" The words were harsh and there was a white line around his mouth. "Is he good-looking? You're not thinking about that muscle-bound son of a bitch? Because if you are, you can forget it. You heard me, Whitney. You can just—''

She grasped his face between her hands. "Hush a minute. Did you listen to yourself, Dean? Did you listen to what you were saying? You don't want me to be with another man any more than I want you to be with another woman. Why do you suppose that is? Why do you think it hurts so much to think of either of us with someone else?''

He pulled away and stood up, turning his back on her. "What was that?" he asked, his voice rough. "Some kind of game?''

"No," she denied, moving to stand directly behind him. "I don't play games with you. I wouldn't do that. You know why, Dean? You're too important to me. I'm not afraid to admit how I feel. I love you. I've loved you for as long as I can remember. If anyone was playing games it was you.''

When he swung to face her, she knew he was going to deny it.

"Yes," she said before he could speak. "You. You've been pretending that we're having an affair. A casual, disposable thing. And that's not the truth, is it?''

A shudder shook through him. "No, it's not. You're right. What I feel for you is not casual. Not disposable. I love you, Whitney."

With a little squeal of relief, she threw her arms around his neck and kissed him.

He responded immediately, drawing her close to run his hands urgently over her body, then seconds later he pulled back from the kiss. "Whit—"

"What's the matter?" she breathed against his cheeks. "Why did you stop? That was some of my best stuff. Better men than you have crumbled under the weight of that particular kiss." She smiled and shook her head. "I'm lying of course. There is no better man than you." She took his hand from her shoulder and held it against her cheek. "And now that you've admitted you love me, you're perfect."

"I couldn't very well deny it," he said with a strange, choking laugh. "Not after making a fool of myself when I thought you were going to see someone else. I've loved you since you were sixteen years old, but all these years I've been trying to convince myself that it was something else. Desire, respect, admiration, sincere liking. When you combine all those things with the feeling that I'm not quite complete unless you're with me, you get love. All along it was love. It's not something I asked for, and it's not something I can deny, either."

A moment after joy began to spread through her like wildfire, the full sum of his words began to penetrate. He had made the admission reluctantly, regretfully, as though he didn't want to love her, but there wasn't anything he could do about it.

She hid her face against his shoulder, unwilling to let him see how much it hurt, knowing that he wasn't as happy about their love as she was.

When she had gained control of her emotions, she pulled back slightly and met his eyes. "You think you could do better?" she asked, one brow raised. "Well, let me clue you in, dumpling. You can't. You won't ever find anyone who could love you better than I can. I've had a lot of practice. After all, I've been doing it all my life. And that's your fault. If you weren't so wonderful, I wouldn't love you to the bottom of my toes. Take away the part of me that loves Dean and there wouldn't be much left. Nothing but an incredibly beautiful shell."

He laughed, pulling her closer. He was holding her so tightly, she could barely breathe. There was an urgent feel to the embrace. A desperate feel.

"What's wrong?" she whispered. "Something's scaring you. Why can't you talk to me about it?"

"Nothing...no really, it's nothing." He smoothed kisses across her forehead. "I was just thinking of something your mother said. She said I was your rebellion."

He moved away from her. "It made sense, Whitney. And don't try to tell me you haven't made it your life's work to tick off the Harcourts. Your apartment, your new job, those things aren't just about getting close to your father. When you came here you didn't just separate yourself from people, from a way of life. You left everything Harcourt behind.''

''So?''

''So maybe I'm part of that. An affair with me is certainly something all your relatives would disapprove of.''

''Not all of them. Baby thinks you're sexy as hell.''

When he didn't respond, she drew in a slow breath, trying to sound calm when she really wanted to scream at him. She had never heard anything so ridiculous.

''Okay...okay,'' she said in irritation. ''You may be right about the apartment and the job. I don't know. I haven't thought about it. But even if you're right, it doesn't have anything to do with how I feel about you. I wanted you when I was a good little Harcourt—''

''You were never a good little Harcourt.'' A hint of a smile was twitching at his lips.

''As I was saying,'' she said with a quelling look. ''I wanted you when I was a Harcourt and now that I'm a full-fledged Grant, I still want you. I still love you. If I found out tomorrow that I'm adopted and am really heir to the British throne, I would still feel the same way. My love for you is *not* a rebellion. It's a given, a constant, a fact of life.''

He jerked her back into his arms and just before his mouth covered hers, she heard him say, ''Maybe it's enough. Sweet heaven, let it be enough.''

Chapter Twelve

"What are you thinking about so hard?" Dean asked.

Whitney raised her head off his chest and looked up at him. "Lloyd...Daddy. You don't know how often I've almost called him that. I was just thinking that if I had him—as a father rather than a friend—I would have everything I've ever wanted."

She ran her fingers in an absentminded caress over his bare thigh. "I know I've got to tell him soon, but every time I try, something always stops me. Something in him. But it's not just that blasted wall he puts up. Something—I don't know. It's a kind of darkness or a sadness that comes over him when he thinks about the past."

Dean settled her more closely against him. "From what the others say, he's opened up a lot since you came here. But I know what you're talking about. There's still a part of him that's sealed up tight...and whatever's in there isn't giving him an easy time."

She sighed. "It's like that story, *The Lady or the Tiger*? I don't know what's behind the closed door and it scares me. I'm afraid I'll hurt him or even lose him, simply because I don't know what I'm dealing with."

He smoothed the hair from her forehead. "What are you going to do?"

"I'm going to tell him." She smiled, then kissed his chest, his neck and his chin. "I didn't get where I am—in the arms of the sexiest, most adorable man in the country—without taking chances. I've never believed in 'if only.' There's no way I'm going to spend the rest of my life regretting something I didn't do. So I'm going to do it, and if I screw up, I'll deal with that, too."

It was a good decision. She was sure of that. And during the next few days Whitney had plenty of opportunities to tell Lloyd that she was his daughter. On one occasion, the words were halfway out of her mouth before she changed her mind and coughed instead.

She had known that getting to the sticking point wouldn't be easy, but sometimes it seemed almost impossible.

On Saturday night several people from the toy factory gathered at her apartment to watch a rerun of *The*

Magnificent Seven on cable. It was a noisy, entertaining evening, especially after the movie was over. All the men in the group pretended they were gunslingers—Whitney had people dying all over her living-room floor—while the women huddled around the table and tried to talk over the noise.

They had all chipped in to have pizza delivered, but Whitney—with the help of a downtown bakery—provided dessert and coffee, and it was well after midnight before her guests, with the exception of Dean and Lloyd, finally said good-night and left.

Whitney made another pitcher of iced tea—the air-conditioning had gone out again—and the three of them sat around the kitchen table talking.

"I really admire the way you hint to your guests that it's time to leave, Mary," Lloyd said, his lips shaking as he tried to sound sincere. " 'Do you think this rash on my leg is contagious?' may not be subtle, but it was certainly effective. I've never seen a room clear so fast."

Dean chuckled. "Oh, she's always been inventive. Did I tell you about the time—"

Whitney groaned. "Please, Dean. Do you know how many times I've heard those stupid words in the past few weeks? The only reason Lloyd doesn't throw up when he hears them is he either has a strong stomach or he's brain-dead. Or maybe he's simply too much of a wuss to tell you to zip it."

"Zip it," Lloyd told her. "Go ahead, Dean. Tell your story."

"As I was saying," he said, giving Whitney a smug look, "she was in eighth grade— No, I think it was the seventh. Anyway she forgot to study for this really important history test. I think she was out messing around with her horse or something."

"I wasn't 'messing around' with him," Whitney said, her voice indignant. "He had a cough. Ben was my very first horse. I couldn't study for a dumb test when Ben might have been coming down with pneumonia."

"It wasn't a cough. He just snorted funny."

She laughed. "I think he had enlarged adenoids," she admitted.

"What about the test?" Lloyd prompted.

"It was true-false. Since she hadn't studied, she didn't know any of the answers and figured she would fail it anyway, so she decided what she needed was a system."

Remembering, Whitney groaned again and stood up to walk to the sink where the party dishes were soaking. "You are evil and must be destroyed," she muttered under her breath as she dipped her hands into the soapy water.

"What kind of system?" Lloyd asked, his voice filled with anticipatory laughter.

"Well, at first she was going to mark True on all the questions—she figured she'd get at least half of them right that way—but she decided that was too dull, so she answered to the tune of the 'Blue Danube.' True ... True ... True ... True ... True ... False, false ... False, false."

When the two men roared with laughter, Whitney threw a handful of suds at them, lifting a chin in haughty indignation. "I passed it, didn't I?"

"You're kidding," Lloyd said as he struggled to catch his breath.

Dean shook his head wryly. "Whitney has always had the luck of the devil, she . . ."

When the words faded away into silence, Whitney looked over her shoulder in curiosity. The two men sat at the table staring at each other. Dean's expression was pained and Lloyd had gone white.

"Whitney?" the older man whispered.

Dean switched his gaze to her. "I'm sorry. God, honey, I'm so sorry."

She was still staring at Lloyd, taking in the stunned look on his face. "No," she said softly, "don't be sorry. It had to happen sooner or later."

Lloyd slowly turned his head to look at her, taking in each detail of her face. *"Who are you?"* he rasped out.

She shrugged, tightening her lips to stop their trembling. "Whitney Daryn Grant," she said, her voice barely audible. "Your daughter?"

As father and daughter stared at each other, Dean rose to his feet and walked out of the kitchen.

Lloyd didn't seem to notice. Even when he rose to his feet, he never took his eyes from her face.

Whitney simply stood by the sink, waiting for him to say something, waiting for him to take even one step toward her. But seconds later he turned and without a word, walked out of the kitchen.

The move took her by surprise and a couple of seconds passed before she was able to move. She pushed away from the Formica counter that had been supporting her and ran, catching up with her father as he reached the front door.

"Don't!" she called out. "You can't— Don't you dare walk out on me again. *Don't you dare.*"

For a moment Whitney thought he was going to ignore her shouted demand, but he paused with his hand on the doorknob, his back to her.

She drew in a deep breath and pushed the hair from her forehead. "You don't owe me love," she said, her voice low and shaken. "Or loyalty. You don't have to care... you don't even have to like me. But damn it, you owe me some kind of explanation. I want you to tell me why you left. I want to hear why you never even once got in touch with me. Why, for God's sake, did you let me spend my whole life thinking my father was *dead?*"

As she stood staring at his stiff back, a violent shudder shook through him. "Your mother wanted it that way," he said finally, the words flat, almost indifferent.

Moving forward, Whitney leaned her shoulder against the wall beside the door, trying to see his face, needing to know if his features matched his impassive voice. But his head was bowed, his expression hidden.

"And you just said, 'Gee, that sounds like a great idea. Let's tell the kid I died'?"

He shook his head. "You don't understand. I was in no position to make demands. It had to be her way." He drew in an unsteady breath. "I put her through hell. I—I *had* to do what I could to make it up to her. She said you would both be better off, and— I wasn't feeling too good about myself at the time, so I could see her point."

"What happened?" she whispered in desperation. "Tell me, Daddy. Why did you think we would be better off if you were dead?"

He raised his head slowly, turning it slightly in her direction, then winced as though the sight of her face hurt him. Shifting his position, he leaned against the door and closed his eyes.

"I don't suppose you remember," he said slowly, "but in Winnetka, I had a decent job. Not a great job, but a decent one. I was one of a dozen bookkeepers who worked for a big company. A profitable company." He opened his eyes and met hers squarely. "Anne gave up so much to marry me. She gave up everything, Mary... Whitney."

He paused, swallowing with difficulty. "We went to San Antonio once after we were married. Just once. But once was enough. I guess you know better than anyone how she was raised. She had everything money could buy. I could see how it hurt her, struggling to make ends meet, never having enough money for the luxuries she was used to. It was wearing her down...and seeing that was killing me. I—I just wanted to give her some of the things she deserved."

He shook his head. "I'm not trying to make excuses for what I did. I just want you to understand why I did it."

"You took money?"

He nodded, exhaling a slow, shuddering breath. "I embezzled almost fifty thousand dollars. When the loss was discovered... when they came to the house and arrested me— It was on a Saturday. You were upstairs sleeping. You know, even now, after all these years, when I close my eyes, I'm there again, living it over again. And the look in her eyes tears at me just like it did the first time. It just about destroyed her, Whitney. She couldn't take the shame. She was terrified that the people back home in San Antonio would find out that her husband was a criminal. She— She stayed until I was sentenced, then she was gone."

He shrugged, the movement weary. "I think she told her brother, but everyone else thought I was dead. I had been in prison for almost a year when she wrote and told me what she had done. She explained why she thought it was best if I didn't try to see you when I got out.

"It wasn't an easy thing for me to accept. It— It ate at me. God, I almost came after you dozens of times. Once I even got all the way to San Antonio. I had convinced myself that no one had the right to keep us apart, not even your mother. You were my daughter, and I had a right to at least see you, to make sure you were all right, to make sure you were happy." He drew in a slow breath. "But I couldn't do it. When it came to the sticking point, I just couldn't do it. I thought about the way people reacted when they found out I'd been in prison... And sooner or later, they always find out. You don't know, you can't imagine what it's like, a particular look in their eyes, a certain something in their tone. And I knew it would be much worse for you. You would find yourself torn between loyalty and resentment. I couldn't do that to you... You see that, don't you, baby? I couldn't let my sins ruin your life. I had to accept that what Anne said was the truth. I gave up all rights to you the day I decided to take money that didn't belong to me."

When Whitney began to shake her head in violent rejection of the idea, he touched her face. "Your mother did it for you. Don't you understand? There was no stigma attached to a father who had died in a boating accident. But a father who was serving five to seven in a correctional institution? People can be so cruel. She was simply trying to protect you."

"She had no right," she whispered tightly. "She *had no right*. I grieved for you every day of my life. She knew that. She knew how I cried for you. Dear God, Daddy, she knew I would rather have you than all the Harcourts in the world. Mother *knew* that."

"Hush, baby." He reached out and wiped the tears from her cheeks. "If you have to blame someone, blame me. I was stupid and weak."

"Everyone makes mistakes," she rasped out. "You don't throw people away like trash... no matter what they've done. She should have been stronger. Together, the three of us could have stood up to anything. She should have—"

"You can't get away from the way you're made," he interrupted. "Your mother has a tremendous amount of pride. I've always loved that about her. Oh yes," he added when her head jerked up in surprise, "I still love her. I never stopped. And I think, in her own way, she still loves me. But we can never be together. One moment of weakness in me and a world full of pride in her make it impossible."

"It's false pride. *Harcourt* pride."

"To you and me maybe, but to Anne it's everything. It's the way she was raised. If you're a Harcourt, you're somebody. They have a set of standards that are too rigid to live up to, but they spend their lives trying."

"They spend their lives pretending," she said, spitting out the words with contempt. "And they hurt people who get in the way of that stupid pretense. They always— They hold on to the counterfeit and toss away the real thing."

He put his arms around her, and she cried softly against him, thinking what a terrible waste it all was. Such a sad, foolish waste of love.

A moment later she clutched his arm tightly. "You won't leave me again? You'll let me be a part of your life. You'll be a part of mine. I—I used to talk to you in my daydreams, you see. I built all kinds of wild fantasies around a phantom father. But I can't make do with fantasies anymore. I need the real thing. I need a real live father in my life. And we— We're friends, aren't we?" She tried to smile, but it was a pitiful effort. "You can't ever have too many friends."

"Maid Mary," he murmured. "Your mother knows you're here? In Dallas? With me?"

She nodded.

"I guess that's why she hasn't written lately."

"She *writes* to you?" she asked in disbelief.

"Every week for almost twenty years." His lips twisted in a sad little smile. "She never mentions the past. She would tell me about you... not in any great detail, but that you were doing fine and growing like a weed, that kind of thing. They're the kind of letters you'd write to a pen pal." He shook his head. "It took me a while to get used to that, but if there's one thing I've learned, it's that you can get used to anything. Anything."

"She hasn't written because she burned all your letters to keep me from seeing them. Knowing Mother, she didn't have your address written down anywhere." She gave a short, harsh laugh. "Pen pal letters? You should have written us off years ago and gotten yourself a new family."

He smiled. "I have a family. You and your mother were never out of my thoughts, never out of my heart. And now that you're here, now that you've let me into your life, it's enough. By God, it's more than I ever dreamed of."

He kissed her forehead, then reached for the doorknob. "I think we both need some time alone now. We can talk again tomorrow." He smiled down at her. "We have a lot of catching up to do, Maid Mary."

When the door closed behind him, Whitney turned and saw Dean standing in the darkened hall that led to the bedroom.

"You heard?" Whitney asked him.

He nodded, a short, jerky movement. "Tough. Tough on you. Tough on him."

Something was wrong. She couldn't read his expression, but there was something about his voice that worried her. It was dull, lifeless, almost as though he had suddenly turned off all feeling.

A shiver took her off guard, shaking through her violently, and although the room was hot, she felt a sudden chill that worked from the inside out.

When he walked into the living room and sat in an armchair, moving as though he were tired, she followed him.

"What are you thinking?" she said, giving a nervous little laugh. "You sound peculiar."

He shrugged. "I was thinking about how he's wasted his life. He's spent the past twenty years standing in the shadows. Not dead, not quite alive."

She sat on the floor at his feet. "It must have been awful for him. Much worse than for me. I didn't know he was alive, but he knew that Mother and I existed. He knew that we were alive, and he couldn't reach us. He blames himself, you know. He made a stupid mistake, so he feels it's only right that he pay for it for the rest of his life. But the biggest mistake wasn't his. It was Mother's."

"No, you're wrong," he said quietly. "Your mother did the only thing she could do under the circumstances."

Her eyes widened in surprise. "You're defending her? She deprived me of a father, but that's nothing to what she did to him. She deprived Daddy of his *life*. And you're defending her? How can you take her side?"

"I'm not taking anyone's side. I'm simply saying that she was caught in a no-win situation. They both were. And maybe I'm saying the biggest mistake was Lloyd's. Not the embezzling. His mistake was getting involved with her in the first place. He should have known it wouldn't work."

Whitney was suddenly afraid. And the fear wasn't caused just by what he was saying. With his attitude, with the look on his face, he seemed to be intentionally putting a distance between them.

The next moment, he stood up abruptly. "We don't need to talk about this tonight. You're wrung out. You're too emotional."

"Too emotional? *Too emotional?*" She pushed a trembling hand through her hair. Confusion and a sudden, unexplainable panic were making it impossible to think. "I just got my father back. Surely that entitles me to a little emotion." She rose to her feet. "But this isn't about my father or what happened twenty years ago, is it? There's something else. Something that's eating at you."

He stared at her for a moment, then turned toward the door. "Let's put this off until tomorrow."

"Don't leave." The words were frantic as she moved quickly to stand behind him, placing a hand on his shoulder. "Why does everyone keep trying to leave me? Dean—Dean, you've got to talk to me."

He swung around, his movements stiff and awkward, his dark eyes blazing with anger. Then, as she watched, the fire died and there was no feeling there at all. "I don't know what you want me to say," he said quietly.

"For starters, you can tell me why, in your evaluation of my mother and father's situation, you left out love." Her voice was shaking with intensity. "You implied— You think that Daddy should never have married Mother. But you didn't say a word about the fact that they loved each other. And it wasn't a wimpy little love, either, Dean. It was strong enough, deep enough, to survive twenty years of separation. That means something. Surely that means something. That they— They truly love each other, Dean."

"And where did that get them?" he asked, his voice rough. "In the long run, this time-defying love you're talking about wasn't worth a flipping, secondhand doughnut. They loved each other in the past, they apparently still love each other, but did that change anything?" He gave a short, harsh laugh. "Their lives are a total mess, but by God they *love.* Big deal."

His anger was all out of proportion, and she couldn't understand what was behind it. All she knew was that she was so scared, she was shaking with it.

"Love *is* a big deal," she said in a hoarse whisper. "I love you, and to me that's a big deal."

He laughed again, but it wasn't a laugh born of amusement or happiness. It was filled with anger and regret and something that seemed very close to self-contempt.

"Yes, you love me," he rasped. "And that only makes it worse."

He turned his back on her and before she could stop him, he moved across the room and walked out the front door.

She pressed a trembling hand to her mouth. Dear God, what was happening? The words, the emotions... It felt so final, and she couldn't understand how it had happened.

Only minutes earlier she had truly believed they were happy. She thought they were going to spend the rest of their lives together. Now, standing alone in her living room, she felt as though she had lost him, and she didn't know how or why.

Turning back to the empty room, she moved a few steps, then sank down on the floor. She leaned back against the couch, her eyes closed as she finally let the tremors take control.

She didn't know how long she had been sitting there before she felt a hand on her head. Opening her eyes, she found Lloyd kneeling beside her, compassion and love in his eyes as he stroked her hair.

"I saw Dean leave," he said. "I saw what he looked like, and I figured now would be a good time to start being a father." He gathered her into his arms, and pulled her up to sit beside him on the couch. "Don't cry so hard, baby. You'll make yourself sick."

"I love him, Daddy," she said in a helpless whisper. "I love him so much."

He rocked her back and forth in his arms. "I know. I know you do, baby. And Dean loves you, too, but he's running scared right now. He can't think straight. You and I see him as an intelligent, successful man, but Dean sees something different. He said he came from the wrong side of the tracks. He was talking about Trash Town, wasn't he? You don't simply forget a lifetime of humiliation, insults and snubs, Whitney. Take my word for it. There's a part of Dean that will always be that boy from Trash Town."

He pushed the hair from her forehead and met her eyes. "Dean's talked to me about his past. Not much, but enough for me to know what it must have been like for him. Honey, he's scared to death that someday, somehow, he'll turn into his stepfather."

When she made a noise of disbelief, he said, "You're right...you're right. It's crazy. But what's locked inside a person's head isn't always open to reason. Dean knows, he's been taught, that bad boys from the slums don't mix with nice girls from millionaire row."

"That's stupid. It's *insane!* He can't really believe that. He *knows* me, Daddy. Better than anyone. He knows there is no one else in the world for me but him. And I know him," she said, her voice not shaking quite as much now. "If he really is thinking that...that *garbage,* then he needs me. He needs me to be beside him, reminding him of who and what he is—the best man I've ever known or am ever likely to know."

Lloyd looked away from her, and releasing her, he stood up and walked a few steps away, his back to her. "It's like watching a rerun," he said. "She loved me like that. She loved me so much."

Scrambling to her feet, she walked around him, facing him. "*I am not my mother!* Why can't anyone see that? I'm not even a Harcourt. I'm *me*. Whitney Daryn Grant. And the only way that will ever change is if I add Russell to the end of it. No other name will work." She drew in a steadying breath. "My love is tougher than hers, Daddy. *I'm* tougher. I don't give up when things get bad."

She moved away from him, forcing her breathing to return to normal, willing the blood to stop pounding in her temples. When she was calmer, she said, "Maybe if I had been raised like Mother I'd feel the way she does. I can't imagine it, but I suppose anything's possible. But the thing is, I wasn't raised that way. They tried to turn me into a Harcourt... you wouldn't believe how hard they tried, but I had Dean. He was there to teach me about life. Real life, not the fake Harcourt version of it.

"If Dean were thrown in jail, if he were disgraced in the eyes of the whole world, where do you think I'd be? Beside him, Daddy. Right beside him. *Always*." She said the word with such fierce intensity that her voice shook. "Just like I would have been beside you if anyone had bothered to let me know what was happening."

She shook her head. "It didn't work for you and Mother. I accept that. But it *has* worked for others.

People from different backgrounds make it work every day. If it's important...if it's the most important thing in your life, you can make it work."

She gave a broken laugh and wiped at the tears with the backs of her hands. "You think it's over, and Dean thinks it's over, but I know different. I don't give up, Daddy. You might as well know that about me right now. I've been waiting for Dean since I was a little girl and I won't settle for anything less. I'll go after him and I'll stay with him. I'll annoy him and exasperate him and make him madder than hell, but I'll stay. I'll stay and eventually I'll wear him down."

Her laugh was stronger this time. "I can be pretty irresistible when I put my mind to it. Dean knows that. He won't like it, but he won't have any choice in the matter. Because I'll stay with him until...until he tells me he doesn't love me anymore."

"Then I guess you'll have to stay forever...because I'll never be able to say that, Whitney."

The quiet words had her swinging around toward the door. Dean was standing not three feet away from her, his eyes trained on her face, examining, searching, with feverish intensity.

"You heard?" she asked, raising her chin in a defensive movement.

He nodded. "I heard." He glanced at Lloyd. "I think she means it."

Lloyd smiled. "Looks like it to me. You told me she was a tenacious devil. You would have done well to remember that.'' He kissed Whitney on the forehead. "See you tomorrow, my Maid Mary."

"Good night, Daddy." Her voice was distracted as she continued to study Dean's face, feeling the gap between them miraculously growing smaller.

When the door closed behind Lloyd, Dean moved closer, his palms turned up in a helpless gesture. "Lloyd was right," he said quietly. "I was running scared, Whit. I was afraid of possibilities. Of what *might* happen. I was afraid of what the future *might* bring. God, baby, I was scared to death of losing you someday."

He paused to draw in a deep breath, his head thrown back, his eyes closed. "I had this hellish vision— I could see myself holding on to you, begging you to stay, offering to subtract years from my life if it would just keep you with me."

He met her eyes. "That damned vision took over, Whit. And then, when I was walking away from you, it suddenly occurred to me what a fool I was. I was throwing away your love—the only thing in the world that matters—because I didn't think I could face having it taken away from me at some indeterminate point in the future."

"Stupid...stupid." The words were a caress as she moved into his arms and began to smooth her lips across his face.

"Yes, it was stupid. Maybe what we have together will fall apart someday. Maybe there's pain ahead, but if I can have you until then, it'll be worth it." He framed her face with his hands. "I hope you think so, too, Whitney. There are things you don't know about me. You don't know—" He shook his head. "There are ugly parts, black parts... I don't want you to get hurt. I've always wanted the best for you. Only the best. You have to know right now that living with me, loving me, won't be easy."

Whitney reached up and touched his face, soothing away the troubled lines. Dean's insecurities weren't going to go away overnight. Maybe they would never disappear completely. They would both have to work at keeping the intimacy alive. The intimacy of mind, body and spirit. But she didn't doubt for a moment that they would make it. Loving Dean was an idea she would never give up on.

"I think I can handle it," she told him as she snuggled closer. "I'm made of pretty tough stuff. And I've always liked a problem I can really sink my teeth into." She bit him lightly on the chin. "Loving you... being there when you need me... learning to be the best wife this planet has ever seen... being in your arms every night... having you hold me and touch me and make me go crazy with wanting you... having your babies."

She laughed and there was pure joy in the sound. "You're right, Dean, it won't be easy. But you taught me a long time ago that when something's inevitable, you have to meet it head-on, without complaining, without flinching."

She felt the heat, the need, rising in him, and she pressed her body closer to his. "It's a dirty job," she whispered against his lips, "but somebody's got to do it."

* * * * *

THE DONOVAN LEGACY
from Nora Roberts

Meet the Donovans—Morgana, Sebastian and Anastasia. They're an unusual threesome. Triple your fun with double cousins, the only children of triplet sisters and triplet brothers. Each one is unique. Each one is...special.

In September you will be *Captivated* by Morgana Donovan. In Special Edition #768, horror-film writer Nash Kirkland doesn't know what to do when he meets an actual witch!

Be *Entranced* in October by Sebastian Donovan in Special Edition #774. Private investigator Mary Ellen Sutherland doesn't believe in psychic phenomena. But she discovers Sebastian has strange powers...over her.

In November's Special Edition #780, you'll be *Charmed* by Anastasia Donovan, along with Boone Sawyer and his little girl. Anastasia was a healer, but for her it was Boone's touch that cast a spell.

Enjoy the magic of Nora Roberts. Don't miss *Captivated*, *Entranced* or *Charmed*. Only from Silhouette Special Edition....

SENR-1

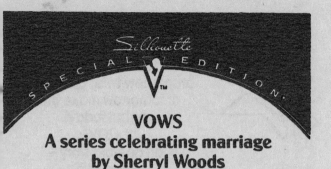

VOWS
A series celebrating marriage
by Sherryl Woods

To Love, Honor and Cherish—these were the words that three generations of Halloran men promised their women they'd live by. But these vows made in love are each challenged by the tests of time....

In October—Jason Halloran meets his match in *Love* #769;

In November—Kevin Halloran rediscovers love—with his wife—in *Honor* #775;

In December—Brandon Halloran rekindles an old flame in *Cherish* #781.

These three stirring tales are coming down the aisle toward you—only from Silhouette Special Edition!

SESW-1